Mel's Revenge

Copyright

Dedication

This book is dedicated to my loving husband without whom I would never have been able to write this. Also to my children for allowing me to get on with writing and drawing, while simultaneously providing me with more material… perhaps this is a vicious cycle?
If you liked Mel's Revenge please leave me a nice review on Amazon.
If you didn't like it, please don't leave a review, because no one likes haters.

In the Classy Crime Series

It helps to have read these stories in order, but it's not essential

Chapter 1

The phone rang just as Mel was about to start making dinner.

"Hello, is that Meline Sanderson?"

"Yes?"

"Hi Meline. My name is Frank Simpson. I work for your Internet provider as a technician. I'm sorry to inform you but your computer's Internet security has been breached. We need to access your computer terminal, to make sure that the hackers cannot access any of your personal information."

Frank's voice seemed vaguely familiar to Mel, as though she had spoken to him before in passing. She hated technical stuff and the thought that she had been targeted with hackers was beyond irritating.

"Fantastic," Mel muttered, looking over at the messy kitchen bench where the half made pizza dough sat waiting for her to finish it.

"I'm sorry madam, what was that?" Frank asked.

"Nothing, how long is this going to take?"

"Just a few minutes. We just need to get your ISPN number, password and a few other details to confirm that you are Meline Sanderson. Then we need to make sure the hackers can't access any personal information. We can do the rest remotely," Frank informed her.

Mel sighed, and resigned herself to an afternoon of tech problems.

Knowing how annoying the tech guys were at her work, Mel went down the path of least resistance. She divulged all the necessary information, hoping she could get on with the gourmet pizza she had planned.

Surprisingly, it did only take a few minutes to give the technician all the information he needed, and Mel was able to get back to making dinner quickly.

The apartment doorbell rang two minutes later and Mel huffed in frustration,

looking up from the pizza dough she had just started to knead.

"Coming," Mel yelled, grimacing at her dough-covered hands. She knew whoever was waiting could hear her just fine through the thin door.

The bell rang once more, as Mel did her best to quickly clean her hands.

Sal and Di would arrive in another hour and they would be expecting Mel to have made dinner for their movie night.

Opening the door, Mel gave a genuine smile to the cute, impatient, male courier and signed for her package.

Five minutes later, Mel wondered why she had even bothered opening the door. The on-line company had promised that this dress was just like the $1200 original. She had tried the original dress on in the actual, 'Real people walk in and try things on,' shop a few weeks ago.

When Mel went into the very exclusive shop in the upmarket district of Wellington's inner city, she was stunned at the price tag on the designer dress.

The dress had looked fantastic on her, despite the derogatory look from the sales clerks. The shop workers had pegged Mel the moment she walked in. They had obviously known she couldn't afford to breathe the air in the shop - let alone buy the dress. Unfortunately this dress wasn't even close.

The $50 + postage 'Just like the real thing,' on-line version of the dress looked wrong and not just the color. Trying it on in the bedroom a few minutes later proved Mel right. It hung badly and felt itchy.

She looked at herself in the mirror, as she tried to be philosophical about it.

Being average height, and having average colored

brown hair, made her easy to overlook.

Mel had hoped this dress would give her a bit more of the 'wow' factor. She often felt like a walking stereotype for normal and dull.

To combat this she bought loud dresses in vibrant colors, and had her hair styled expensively, in an attempt to make her stand out from the crowd outside of work, while conforming dutifully with dull clothes during business hours.

The dress had seemed too good to be true at the on-line shop at the time.

Maybe she should simply stop trying to get nice things on the cheap.

Nope.

That wasn't any more realistic than her not trying to get a $1200 dress for $50 plus packaging.

She sighed and went back to the kitchen to finish getting dinner prepared.

When the pizza was ready to be cooked, Mel considered her laptop computer currently sitting on the small desk in the next room.

The Internet had recently opened a whole new world for Mel, and after many years of resisting all new technology, she had now jumped in feet first. On-line shopping, price comparisons, local news updates and banking on-line had been an eye-opening experience for her.

Walking to her cozy small bedroom, Mel wasn't sure that all these on-line cheaper bargains had been worthwhile. In fact it might even be a good idea to give shopping a rest for a bit. At least until the credit card bill had been paid in full next month.

Mel booted up her computer to check out the clothing shops website and its refund polices. Unfortunately the website that she'd bought the dress from was no longer active.

After swearing at the computer for a few minutes, and pouting, Mel looked at the dress again, resigning herself to it.

Okay, it wasn't as great as the original, but it was still wearable. Just not comfortable.

Placing the pizza in the oven, she looked around the lounge.

Noticing she had left out scraps of material and her sewing box earlier, she decided to finish the bit of sewing before packing it away.

Her apartment had only one bedroom, but the large living, balcony and fantastic views over Wellington City, more than made up for the small bedroom space.

The apartment building Mel lived in had two apartments per floor, and hers was furnished in wooden varnished furniture and pastel colors on the walls that screamed homemaker. The sparsely furnished, antique furniture and pastel colored quilts that she had made for throws, rested on the couches matched the wall hangings.

A short time later, Mel looked at her half-made quilt and grimaced in frustration.

She loved the money and the notoriety of being the best quilter around, and the local art galleries always wanted more originals. They sold for over five thousand dollars each, but the work just sucked.

It was tedious boring and time consuming.

Mel put the needles and quilt down and got out her sewing machine.

Normally it was hidden in the back of her wardrobe, away from prying eyes, but she still needed it.

Because, despite the 'made by hand' labels she always put on the quilts when they were finished, Mel found that if she wanted her ($5,000.00 each one-of a kind), quilts to look great, without spending months on each one, then the sewing machine was a necessary secret evil.

Although she could sell the quilts regularly, Mel knew

it would never replace the income she got from the insurance company. Mel enjoyed her job, but it meant that she had to be constantly on the lookout for new business, and that meant socializing. So Mel often hosted parties to sway the reps of various companies to change their insurance to her company.

Spending time with people she had no interest in, was time consuming and annoying, but it did bring in the business. Especially when they felt that they had gotten to know Mel as a person through things like the home made quilts, while of course, she make extra money on the side. Quilts, scattered artfully around her apartment, had price tags attached to them. Should anyone question this Mel would simply say that she had been offered a place to exhibit, and was either getting ready for a showing, or she had just taken her work down.

It was a way Mel was able to stand out from the other insurance agents, and bring a human touch to the event. Mel had to get two new clients by the end of the quarter to meet her sales target, and in the current economy it wouldn't be a good idea to fall behind on her targets.

She had started sewing again with the idea that if she did fall behind on her target that she would have some cash to fall back on.

After a short while on the sewing machine, Mel realized she had only ten minutes left, so she started getting ready for a cozy night in watching a movie with her best friends Sal and Di.

They were Mel's only real friends, and they were aware of both the quilt system and the sewing machine, and fully supported it.

Even to the point of telling other people off, for not having been to Mel's exhibitions to support her.

Sure it was unethical, but Mel's day job only paid the main bills and she loved getting the extra income from her 'hobby'.

Mel occasionally wondered about how many lines she was crossing with the quilt sales, but didn't think her white lies were hurting anyone.

Good food, a movie and a few glasses of wine usually made for an evening of fun and laughter.

Mel's new found love of the Internet had provided her with a fabulous new recipe for a low fat feta and spinach pizza topped with pine nuts that looked fantastic. When Sal and Di arrived at the apartment later with chips and the movie, Mel's pizza would be nearly done.

Humming to the music on the stereo while she sorted out the plates for the pizza. Mel thoughts were on the action movie, featuring men with great bodies in tight shirts.

Chapter 2

3 Months Later

"What the HELL do you mean, my card is declined?!!!" Mel demanded, furious.

"I'm sorry, but it's declined," the overweight, unshaven woman serving as a checkout clerk declared.

Mel had stopped off at the local supermarket for groceries. It was Friday night, at the end of a long working week.

A queue was forming behind her, as Mel's face slowly went pink then red. The shop was full of people just like her. Having finished work, they all wanted to get home and relax with one last chore out the way.

A few of them were even glaring at her for holding up the line.

Mel had a week's worth of groceries stacked neatly in the supermarket trolley. The board checkout woman waited patiently for Mel to produce another card.

Unfortunately, Mel was out of cards and she didn't have any cash. Bright red in the face and humiliated, she turned on her heels and walked quickly out of the store. Leaving the fully stacked trolley in front of the checkout clerk, and the people in the queue staring after her rapidly retreating back.

At home, two hours later, Mel was even more confused and slightly stressed out. An on-line check of her bank balance showed all of her accounts overdrawn, and her only credit card maxed out.

The small amount of savings she had carefully looked after for the last few years, was gone. The only reference to the massive, and okay, some not so massive, withdrawals was the reference *"Suck It"* neatly typed on the reference line of the withdrawal section.

"What the hell?"

Mel hastily opened her email in a fresh tab, preparing to send a nasty email to the bank when two new emails appeared in her in-box.

The first e-mail was from her delightful personal banker, asking why she was so massively over drawn.

"You tell me why? Bitch! You're the one who's messed up my accounts!" Mel yelled at the computer screen.

Now was not the time to panic, but Mel didn't really feel that she could wait for a better time.

She looked at the screen, then away at the floor, then back at the screen, hoping for some change in the display to help this make sense.

Mel hated crying in the face of failure, and she despised all heroines that did so in the movies. But somehow hating herself for not being able to figure out something as simple as her own bank balance, made her feel like crying even more.

"Someone is going to pay for this," Mel fumed.

She did her best not to let the angry tears come out, staring at the ceiling as she willed herself to clam down.

Finally, with a hand shaking from fury, Mel moved on to the next email.

It was even more bizarre than the first.

From: suck_it@hotwiredup.com

You thought stealing my money was going to be that easy?
Let's see how you like a taste of your own medicine. I'm going to do to you what you've done to so many others, and then I'm going to do so much more.
Sincerely from
Suck It Up Bitch

Mel sat still at the desk for a minute or two, trying to make sense of it all. When that didn't work, Mel decided to call the most technologically literate person she could think of.

Picking up her cell with a trembling hand, she dialed Sal's number.

"You have insufficient funds to make this call."

The monotone generated voice sounded strangely ominous. She cursed herself for not having a landline. "Hmm."

Mel thought for a long moment.

There was a handful of change on the counter, and maybe some by the fridge. Dashing around her small apartment quickly, she counted the collection of coins that now seemed to represent her current financial worth.

$5.50

Mel swore, using words her mother would be surprised to know that Mel knew. She had enough to catch the bus to Sal and Dianne's apartment, but not back again. What if they weren't home? How the hell could she explain this situation, and not sound completely nuts?

Also, how long did she have before her next pay? A quick look at the calendar eased Mel's mind for a moment, two days before pay day. Mel could survive a few days without money. She could walk to work and make her own lunch.

Let's face it - poor people did it all the time.

Obviously this 'Suck It' guy, had a bad case of mistaken identity. In a few days this will all be sorted out. Then someone would have some serious apologizing to do to her.

Positive thinking, that's the key.

Mel quickly checked her chocolate stash, at the back of the top cupboard.

Yup. Things were going to be fine. She could hold out for a few days, make a few phone calls.

Oh right.

Scratch the phone calls.

She could make a visit to the bank, and the police station. Then this mess would all be sorted out.

Mel pulled herself together as best she could and grabbed her coat. Checking that she had locked the apartment securely, she slowly walked down to the bus stop.

Catching the crowded bus to Sal's house was an eye opener, Mel usually just called a taxi.

The people on the Friday night bus were a noisy, smelly mess of drunkenness. Reeking of body odor and alcohol from the nearby clubs. Some were still bumping and grinding against each other, using the ole at the back of the bus for a seriously bad attempt at pole dancing.

Arriving at the stop near Sal and Di's apartment, Mel felt an overwhelming sense of gratitude that they lived only a few doors down from the bus stop. Their apartment would be cozy and warm after the sticky cold bus. Too late, Mel remembered Di would be out, she had a date.

As Sal was the person who finally convinced Mel to get onto the Internet and helped set up her little laptop, Mel felt as though Sal should be able to offer the best advice. Or at least take some of the blame.

Sal opened the door and looked at Mel in surprise.

"What the hell happened to you?" Sal gasped. "Have you been crying?"

Then Sal paused for a moment, flicking her long blond hair out of her narrowing blue eyes and added,

"Why didn't you call before you came over? You know I hate drop in's."

"Well it's obviously a case of mistaken identity," Sal said a few minutes,
(and two shots of vodka) later.
"Well, duh. Just tell me how to fix it, who do I call? Microsoft, the police, the bank who?" Mel asked refilling

her glass with water this time. The vodka was beginning to go to her head. "You're the most technologically literate person I know."

"That's not a word, honey,"

"You know damn well what I meant. Don't be a pedantic asshat. Just tell me who to call!"

"Um, I don't know." Sal was thoughtful for a moment, swirling the glass of vodka in her hand. "This all started as a mistake, so let's send this 'Suck It' guy a quick email back, and explain the situation."

Mel suddenly felt very stupid.

"Good idea. Can I borrow your computer to send the email now?"

"No," Sal looked pained. "If this guy is as angry as we think he is, then I really don't want my IP address to be on his hit list."

"Oh... right," Mel was silent for a moment.

She understood Sal's position completely, if Mel was in serious trouble, then of course Sal didn't want to be dragged into it too.

"Can I borrow some money, just to get me though the next few days? I really don't want to ask my mother for help."

"Sure," Sal squirmed, obviously wanting to do more for her friend. "Call me and let me know what 'Suck It' says to your email."

"Nope."

Mel paused for a moment, enjoying the shocked, hurt look that flitted across Sal's face, before she let Sal off the hook.

"He screwed my cell up, remember? Otherwise I would have saved the bus fare that I spent coming over here."

"Sorry," Sal looked distraught at Mel's situation.

They were happy to be bitches to the world in general, but to mess with one of them, was to mess with all three.

"Well, I can give a hundred to keep you afloat until this

is all sorted out. I'll need it back by next month though."

Mel nodded her agreement at the terms.

"But, if this guy doesn't back off, then what do I do?" Mel asked. "Microsoft or someplace like that should be able to help shouldn't they?"

They had helped her out a few months ago in a similar situation, surely they would do the same again?

"What?" Sal grinned. She looked like she was laughing at Mel inside. "Honey, they only sell software, they don't deal with hackers."

Mel felt the blood drain from her face.

"So… if someone called, said that they were from Microsoft, and that you needed to protect yourself from hackers then…"

"NO! Honey, you didn't fall for that!" Sal looked horrified, and as though she was trying very, very hard not to laugh. "Tell me you did not give random strangers on the phone any of your information!"

Mel felt her stomach shrivel up like a lemon, and the look on her face said it all to Sal.

"Didn't you ask for identification, or for them to prove who they were? Oh Mel, you've been taken for a serious ride."

Sal had to really struggle to keep a horrified expression on her face, so she wouldn't laugh out loud. "Now all your information is in the wrong hands."

"Well, I couldn't see his ID card over the phone could I?" Mel squeaked.

"Is your name Maple Syrup? Well, it damn well should be, you sap!" Sal gasped out, now completely unable to prevent hysterical laughter from pealing forth.

Mel glared at Sal, and waiting for her to composing herself.

"I think I need another drink," Mel said eventually.

A few hours later, both Mel and Sal were more than

slightly drunk, before they ventured back to the original conversation.

"But, don't you think that the police or the Criminal Investigation Bureau would be able to help me? Or at least explain to this guy, that he has the wrong person?"

"Oh please, Mel," Sal gave her a pitying look "We are talking about the people who have made it okay to video tape your favorite T.V. program so you can watch it later. But then turn around, and then make it illegal to download the same program off the Internet, because you forgot to set the player to record."

Sal hiccuped then continued. "You seriously think they can help? New Zealand IT Law sucks, honey."

"Well, you can't really blame them for not having the policy in place to deal with it. This Internet thing is really creating a whole new type of criminal."

Mel could sympathize with them. It was hard to learn a new skill.

"Mel, you just lost your life savings," Sal said with a raised eyebrow.

Mel paused for a moment.

"You're right. What the hell do we pay them for, if they can't even catch a simple thief?"

Mel went to stand, but the room swam and she realized she was feeling decidedly woozy. "Mind if I stay the night, Sal?"

"Sure, you're way too drunk to walk now, anyway."

Sal got up and smoothly walked to the hallway closet, returning a moment later with some blankets and a pillow.

"Get some sleep, sweetie. It will look better in the morning."

With that, Sal walked to her bedroom and left Mel slumped over on the couch for the night.

The next morning things did not look better for Mel. She was reminded of why she seldom drunk at Sal's house as soon as she opened her bloodshot eyes.

Sal mixed three shots of vodka for every glass of lemonade, and while Mel was a seasoned drinker, Sal's drinks always gave her one hell of a hangover.

"Your red shirt goes well with your eyes," Sal commented early the next morning. Looking happy and hangover free.

"Oh shut up. You're a hardened alcoholic and I'm not," Mel griped. Holding her head in both hands, as she sat at the table. "Something to be proud of, I'm sure."

Breakfast was a fry up - eggs, toast, tomatoes and mushrooms, but no bread as per Sal's new low carb diet.

The perfect hangover food. It was served with juice and coffee. Mel heaped three sugars into her coffee, to Sal's disgust, then tried to force herself to eat more than she usually would.

Mel had very little food left at home, but after her second helping she began to feel the hangover kick in harder, and she was forced to push the plate away.

Di arrived home halfway through Mel's second coffee, her hair looked disheveled and her clothes wrinkled.

Di was tall, blond and easily the best looking of the three friends.

As such, Di regularly used and abused the male population at large. Extorting free dinners and alcohol on a whim.

"Was he everything you had hoped for?" Sal asked, as Di stopped in the doorway to take off her stilettos.

"Mentally no, physically yes," Di grinned like a Cheshire cat.

"Will you see him again?" Sal asked pouring Di a cup of coffee.

Di accepted the cup quickly, taking a seat at the small table.

"Hell. Yes." Di sighed in contentment. "I'm nowhere near through with him." She took a sip of the coffee.

Mel grimaced.

"Sal, feel free to spend the night at my place if you need to."

Mel knew that the sounds of loud, red hot, funky monkey sex coming from the bedroom, would often make breakfast the next day an awkward affair for the two flat mates.

"Thanks," Sal said, with feeling.

"Bring food," Mel added.

After Sal explained to Dianne what had happened to Mel. Mel gained more sympathy and more cash to tide her over, Mel decided to go home and send an email to *'Suck It'*. After she had gone shopping for groceries a second time.

Catching the bus home didn't improve Mel's mood. The drunken crowd from the night before, had morphed into a sad group of weather beaten older people, dressed in layers and hunched against the morning chill.

The smell of urine lingered in the bus, as Mel leaned away from the window, trying to touch as little of the sticky bus seats as possible.

Saturday dragged on-wards, with an unsuccessful visit to the police station in the afternoon.

A fat clerk at the front desk informed her that she would need to speak to her bank to ascertain that there had been a crime, before they could investigate.

Then the bank could give her a letter to take to the police technical department. Who would look at getting her back her life's savings as soon as they could, but only during business hours on weekdays.

Mel ground her teeth and left with bad grace. Stomping out and accidentally shoulder barging a scantily dressed woman. The hooker was being walked into the station with her hands cuffed behind her back, and a policeman behind her.

The prostitute quickly steadied herself, and turned around to yell at Mel. But after glancing at the expression on Mel's face, she continued walking quietly, with the policeman following closely.

The other officers also seemed to be giving Mel a wide berth, as she stalked down the station steps.

The weekend passed quickly. After a second trip to the shops to get much needed basics of flour, rice and cheap in-season vegetables, Mel felt ready to face whoever was messing with her.

A plan of action was always a help.

Mel sent a quick email reply to the *'Suck It'* person.

Hi There

I haven't done anything to you. I think this is a case of mistaken identity. Please check what you are doing and to whom. Because I think you have the wrong person.

From Mel

Then Mel made a point of changing all her passwords on everything she could think of.

The bank, email addresses even her Amazon account, nothing remained the same.

On Monday at lunch time Mel called her bank from her small work cubical.

Only to hit a dead end with the bank clerk. Mel ground her teeth as she tried to keep her patience.

"I'm sorry miss, but the person who made this withdrawal had both your password and identification number. Are you sure you haven't given them out to anyone?"

"Yes, I'm sure!" Mel spoke angrily. ***"Why The Fuck***

Would I Give Anyone My Bank Number?"

"I'm sorry, but I can't speak to you if you use profane language."

The line went dead.

"*Oh Shit,*" Mel said softly.

All around her, Mel imagined she could hear every other person in the office listening.

Even if she left now, she wouldn't have enough time to go to the bank, and back without being late back from lunch, and the way things were going she would need this job badly for quite a while.

After two late lunches with Di and Sal last week, she didn't dare risk a third late lunch.

Well, first thing's first, Mel thought as she brought up the bank website on the computer, and re-changed her passwords a second time. Then brought up her email and did the same. Surely changing every password regularly would keep some one bad out?

Remembering what Sal had told her, Mel also sent another short email to the 'Suck it' email, and explained what had happened as best she could.

Hey Dip-Shit
I didn't take your money, I don't know who did. So please give me my money back and leave me alone!
Sincerely
Mel

Sighing, she looked at the suddenly unappetizing sandwiches she had made for lunch. Wishing she could go out and buy something nicer.

That feeling increased when Mel got home and looked in the kitchen for something to make for dinner. All the ingredients looked like hard work.

Mel's mother would be arriving for dinner soon, and she would expect it ready and waiting. Mel had been very frugal with her shopping trip, wanting to keep as much cash as possible, in case this computer guy kept being stubborn.

The cupboards were, what other people may refer to as, empty. Despite the shopping trip, but Mel knew how to make the basic food last.

Oil, flour, yeast and water meant she could make flat bread and a handful of leftover pizza toppings in the freezer, combined with half a jar of tomato sauce from the fridge made for a good stuffing.

Mel's mother had taught Mel how to survive on the basics, as a matter of necessity when Mel was younger.

Not that Mel or her mother needed to scrape for each meal nowadays, but Mel felt thankful she could remember all that she had learned about cooking on a budget. Mrs Regina Sanderson had been young and single when Mel was born, and so Mel had a choice of potential fathers to get DNA tests from, but she had never bothered. It just seemed like another person to look after if she did find out anyway.

Lately, Regina had decided it would best to marry off Mel to the nearest available male, at the soonest possible time. She suspected that this was because Regina was getting in the mood for grandchildren.

Mel's view was that she was quite happy being single, and should any unsuspecting male that Mother set Mel up with want to visit, then it was game on.

Ten minutes surrounded by the flowers and country patterns in the living room usually had even the strongest of males running for the hills. This also worked on any man that Mel brought home for the night, and she wanted to get rid of the next morning. It was dark when they entered the rooms, and after a night of love making, they awoke to most single men's worst nightmare.

Nothing seemed to make them run faster than the sight of a happy, confident homemaker.

Regina knocked on the door exactly on time. Mel's

mother was an attractive woman in her mid- forties, she stood slightly taller than Mel, at five foot seven, and she still had a slim elegant body always dressed in classic suits. Regina was the type of person who would never go outside, without making sure her bag matched her shoes.

Dinner was at Mel's house on Monday nights at 7pm on the dot.

"You need to settle down, and find a good man to share your life with." Regina informed Mel as soon as they had sat down to eat.

"Why bother? I already have you in my life. Isn't that enough?"

Mel ignored this blatant attempt to control her social life, and served herself a glass of water.

"No."

Mel decided to try a different approach this week.

"You know if I did meet someone, you and I couldn't do this you know."

"Do what?"

"Have dinner once or twice a week to start with. How would that look to a prospective boyfriend?"

Mel smiled at Regina's startled look and started to eat her dinner.

"Just think, I would be getting hot and heavy with some guy, and you would be at home alone, all week long."

Regina looked at Mel eyes wide in horror.

"Wow… even if I used a wire brush, I will never get that mental image out of my head," Regina said finally as she picked up her fork and slowly dug in to her dinner. She was conspicuously quiet for the rest of the evening.

Mel gave a sigh of relief when Regina left a few hours later.

Regina knew something was up with Mel. But she had the good grace, for once, not to try and find out what.

Chapter 3

Tuesday was even worse than Monday.

Unable to sleep at night for worrying and feeling exhausted during the day because of the lack of sleep were making Mel's life a misery

An email came back from *'Suck It'* but it only had two words.

Yeah, Right.

Mel quickly sent back another email trying to get this 'Suck It' to talk to her, thinking that she might be able to open a dialog with them.

Suck It
No really! It's not me! I'm not kidding!
Mel

Mel knew if she could open a conversation with this *'Suck It'* guy she could try reasoning with them, and explain why it wasn't her who had pissed them off.

A visit to the bank during Mel's lunch hour didn't prove productive.

The pretty female teller at the counter, refused to believe Mel hadn't given anyone the passwords to Mel's accounts, and then she informed Mel that the security system they had in place was completely secure.

The manager was called, at Mel's request, and after being taken into a side room Mel was then asked how she was going to pay back her debts.

Calmly explaining to them that if they looked at their records, they could see Mel hadn't over spent on shopping or over indulged in anything really.

But that didn't work out like she had planned.

"You transferred the money electronically, and only left one reference in the subject field called 'Suck It Bitch'."

The manager explained to Mel. "Our system is impenetrable, and we know it was either you, or someone you've given your information to, who transferred your money out. Perhaps you would like to look at some brochures we have."

After refusing to take the flyers with headings like Being Safe On The Internet, AA and Gamblers Anonymous', Mel left the stuffy side office with bad grace.

Later that afternoon, Mel had a brainstorm, and she quickly sent out emailed invites to all her business associates for a party at her place in two weeks' time.

The usual people from work, the new stationary company that she hoped to recruit, and a few other companies that Mel dealt with often.

They almost all replied that they would come. Then Mel decided that more people was better, so she sent a second email, saying partners and spouses were also invited.

That made this party a rare event that the people in the insurance industry wouldn't be able to resist. Mel reasoned that she had a fortnight's time before she ran out of money, thanks to Sal and Di's contribution, and if she got some quilt sales on the night they could pay her in cash.

If she had the cash, then she could keep afloat for a little longer, buying some more time to deal with the mess she was in.

Being the head of a social circle was fun - so long as you didn't have any real friends in it.

The rest of the week passed in a blur for Mel, and by Friday she still had no idea what to do about how to get money.

The chocolate stash was down to one bar, and not only

had Mel been paid, but also sweet talked the accountant at work to advance her another week's pay as well.

Nothing made any difference.

All the payments were done electronically, so Mel's accounts were always maxed out a minute after the pay went in.

Mel didn't know how much longer she could take this. The bank had stood by its original stance, and refused to consider that their system had been hacked.

To make matters worse, without the bank's co-operation, the police were treating Mel like a crackpot.

Then the debt collectors from her credit card company, started to call her at home and work.

Mel had enough money for rent thanks to Sal and Di, so delivered it in person to her landlord on the top floor of her building, but she didn't want to ask for help from her friends again.

Perhaps it was time to tell her mother.

Regina would know how to deal with this.

Nope. Not yet.

It was bad enough to be in this situation, but Regina would only make things worse by getting angry and undoubtedly yelling at the police techs, the one group Mel really needed on her side right now.

Mel changed the passwords twice more, with no success.

On Saturday, Sal and Di arrived at Mel's as usual for movie night.

"Sup, bitch," Sal yelled as she opened the door, at the appointed time, without knocking and plopping herself down on the couch with a sigh.

"Hi guys, dinner will be a minute."

"Got my money yet?" Di greeted Mel with a wicked smile.

"And mine!" Sal called from the couch, where she was putting her purse down.

"Nope, and thanks for giving me just one night without having to think about that, you slapper's," Mel shot back smiling.

She was so glad to see them right now, she could overlook them undoubtedly wanting to rub in how stupid she had been.

"Well, you've only got one week to pay me back. So what's the plan?" Di was still grinning at Mel.

"Dinner is going to be late if you keep talking to me, so put the movie on, bitch."

Di stopped smiling, and looked at Mel critically.

"You don't have a plan do you?" she looked shocked

"Shut up," Mel stopped smiling.

Sal looked over from the couch in astonishment.

"Things are that serious?" She asked Mel.

Mel concentrated on chopping the vegetables, and not stabbing her friends.

"Look, as much as we think this is funny, we are here for you honey."

"Yes but I don't see you brown bagging lunch every day, and getting chased by debt companies." Mel sniffed.

She hated crying, and angry crying was even worse.

The fact that her friends were being nice, instead of making fun of her, just made it sink in how bad things were.

Di and Sal were looking at each other in shock.

"Okay, honey. When you know how to get this bastard, then we will have your back, but we should have a chat about what you've already tried."

"Just so we can see if we can add anything," Sal said not wanting to say Mel may have overlooked something obvious.

Mel explained everything that had happened over the past few weeks. Sal's unspoken thought that Mel had missed something, went unvoiced.

An hour later, dinner was eaten, and no one could think

of anything else to do. So they agreed to sleep on it, and watch the movie as planned, to give everyone a chance to think.

Sal had rented a movie about sparkly vampires, so they could mercilessly mock the actors.

After nearly two hours of telling the movie actors to either put a shirt back on, or the stupid insipid girl to make up her trollop mind, they were all rolling on the floor with laughter.

They all agreed to turn it off before the gooey ending made them regurgitate dinner.

As Di and Sal left, they agreed the only thing to do was to send more emails to Suck It and try and open a dialog for lack of a better plan.

Mel spent the next day sending several more e-mails to *'Suck It'* and had received the same reply.

Yeah right.

Her chocolate stash was down to one bar.

Regina arrived on time Monday evening for dinner.

Unfortunately, Mel had completely forgotten about it, and was sitting on the couch with a warmed bowl of spaghetti straight from the can watching TV, when she heard the knock at the door.

As soon as Mel heard the knock, her treacherous brain clicked into gear.

"Oh, no."

Mel hauled herself painfully off the couch, and dragged her feet to the door.

"Hi Mother. How are you?" Mel said with a fake smile.

Regina looked Mel up and down slowly. "Better than you, I think. Are you going to tell me what's up yet?"

"Um…" Mel looked around at her apartment for the first time in a few days.

Her usually spotless living area was strewn with clothes and dishes, whenever Mel was down the housework came last, and the past few weeks had been very trying. "Well, I'm in a bit of a bind financially, at the moment."

Regina raised an eyebrow as she walked in, and made a point of picking a shirt off the living room chair, and dropping it on the floor, before sitting down.

"I never knew you were bad with money, dear." Regina looked directly at the bowl of spaghetti.

"I'm not." Mel took a breath, and then did her best to explain.

"My bank account keeps getting emptied, and I have no idea how to handle it. I've changed my passwords half a dozen times and it still keeps happening." It came out in a rush.

"So you've been hacked?"

Trust her mother to have a better grasp on technology than most of Mel's friends, and Mel put together.

"Yes, and I can't find out who it is, what they want, or even why they've targeted me." Great now she was whining.

"I see. How much money do you have left?"

"I'm using the cash Sal and Di lent me for rent, but I'm going to fall behind soon."

"Well I don't have an answer, at the moment, for this little set back. So go get changed and let's go for dinner somewhere nice."

Regina looked thoughtfully at Mel. Mel knew that look and felt a small sense of hope surge inside, her mother was a force to be reckoned with in her own right. It was always a good idea to have Regina on her side.

Mel looked down at her sweat pants and t-shirt.

"Sure I'll be a minute."

After Mel had enjoyed a nice dinner, at a more expensive restaurant than she usually would have gone to, and she felt a lot better.

Regina insisted on stopping at a cash machine and withdrawing enough to cover Mel's rent, food and power bills for the next few weeks. As they slowly walked back through the city's night life, they talked about how Mel was managing the situation.

Regina was intrigued to hear that Mel's phone had also been taken over, and her credit cards had been maxed out. Not to mention the pay being removed from Mel's account as soon as it had gone in.

"I am having trouble with anything Internet or technical. Frankly I'm wishing we still paid in cash for everything," Mel sighed, as her hatred for all things I.T. based renewed.

"I have no idea how to help you, honey." Regina finally admitted, to Mel's disappointment. "An ordinary hacker might have gotten your money, but not after you changed all the passwords at the same time, and the fact that your phone was also affected has me stumped. Can I buy you a new book, to take your mind off things?"

Mel looked at the bookshop they were passing, the current flavor of the month was a gray covered book.

"No thanks I'm more of an M&M girl, than an S&M girl. Thanks anyway though."

"We'll buy you some M&Ms then, and call it a night," Regina said with finality. She knew how important the chocolate stash was to Mel. "As soon as we find this guy, there is going to be hell to pay. I want his balls nailed to the wall."

Mel laughed as they continued walking home.

Next Saturday night, the party at Mel's apartment had kicked off like all the others. It was a loud and vibrant affair, with the usual mixture of clients and insurance sales people.

The addition of partners and significant others, had the

people in the insurance industry mingling, and chatting about non-work related subjects for a change. Insurance company people, and clients hanging out together was always a small group affair. Even in a larger city like this.

At most there were seven large companies in Wellington, and only a few people from each company would be invited to Mel's. Of course, Mel would never invite a company if they were competing for the same clients, and she always invited her most satisfied customers, so they could help with the good marketing of her own company.

Mel called her usual catering company to deliver the standard order, and they had accepted, to Mel's relief, without asking the question of how she was going to pay. They had assumed that she would pay as usual, at the end of the month.

Although she was still at a loss with how to go forward in finding out who was behind her current problems, Mel had thought of several things to do to the culprit once she found out.

She had planned that later this evening, when the alcohol had a chance to kick in, the music would be turned up, they would push the furniture against the walls for dancing. Mel had made sure her camera and cell phone with camera and video function were fully charged. Just in case she needed any favors in the next few weeks.

Chances are, the way things had been going, she would need a lot of favors and soon.

Inviting the partners of her work mates had given Mel a new insight to her co-workers.

Opening the door for the tenth time, revealed her boss Mark and another man, arm and arm holding a bottle of wine.

"Hello, Mark. Welcome to the party."

"Hello, Mel. This is my partner David." Mark managed to get out before David flounced into the room.

"Halloo. Darrrling. It is just *such* a delight to meet you at long last."

David kissed Mel on each cheek, as he came in the apartment and looked around critically. "I just love the space in here." He declared loudy gaining the attention of everyone in the room.

Mel hadn't even known her quiet, uptight boss was gay. She stared in astonishment as Mark's boyfriend sashayed his way around the room introducing himself to everyone.

Mark shrugged, and made his way to the kitchen bench that Mel had set up as a bar.

David was definitely the extrovert of the couple, Mel realized, as he talked loudly with jazz hands, as Mark made their drinks.

Mel made another drink for her co workers with Mark and made small talk, while she noticed several new faces in the crowd of nearly thirty, crammed into the apartment.

She had expected to see a few new people, with the invites to include partners, but one man in particular seemed to stick out.

He looked around Mel's age and well-dressed, but slightly out of place with the other people, as though he hadn't expected to be here.

The newcomer didn't chat to many other people for long before moving on to the next group. He had come in with a larger group earlier, when Mel was stuck talking to a couple, and he had also brought a nice wine, so Mel hadn't been able to introduce herself yet.

Mel decided that he must be from the new stationery company she had hoped to land the insurance contract for. They hadn't replied to her email, but that didn't mean anything. Mel made her way over checking him out as she went.

The man was cute, almost hot, but with a slightly geeky demeanor. Hair casually mussed, he looked just short of six foot and had nice broad shoulders, but he was lean enough to make Mel instantly want to give him a hot meal… or something else. Dark hair framed his face and strong jaw.

Mel realized she was staring at him and quickly looked away.

Mel was quickly glad that the last few days of next to nothing to eat, had allowed her to drop a few pounds and fit into her skinny black pants with red backless halter top for the evening.

"Hi there," Mel tried not to purr too much, as she walked up to him. "How are you enjoying the party?"

"It's great," he replied smiling down at her. "I was kind of hoping to meet the hostess, and thank her for the invite. I understand it's kind of rare for partners to be invited."

Mel's smile widened, and took on an almost predatory look, she didn't want to come on too strong with a potential client.

But if he was game then so was she.

"So you're not here as a husband or significant other then?" She asked quickly covering all the bases.

"No, just looking to blow off some steam and have some fun." He replied folding his arms and looking at Mel with interest. "Do you know where she is?"

"I'm Mel," Mel replied enjoying the way his eyes widened.

"Seriously, you're Mel?" He looked a little shocked. "I have to say you weren't what I pictured."

"Huh? What did you think an insurance consultant would look like?" Mel asked puzzled.

He seemed to take a moment to process before replying.

"A little more uptight, and definitely not as cute." He eventually said, after staring at her for a long moment. "I know this is a little forward, but do you have anywhere we can talk?"

"Um. No." Mel was keen, but not that keen.

"I didn't mean that. Not that you're not…" He was easily flustered.

It was so cute.

"Look, I have a company that needs to change insurances, and I heard your company might be what I'm looking for. But I need to ask some questions first."

"OK," Mel said, relaxing and remembering her well-rehearsed sales pitch. "How about on the balcony?"

It would be a few hours before people were drunk enough for her to take photos or buy quilts anyway.

"Sure," He smiled back easily.

"I'll just be a moment." Mel smiled as he went through the small crowd to the balcony door.

"Mark, I think The Shed is here for an insurance bid," Mel said as she passed David and Mark at the kitchen bar.

"The stationary place? Great get him over here, if you can't seal the deal I can," said David loudly, as he watched the newcomer waiting for Mel.

Mel laughed at Mark's expression.

"Could you slow down on the alcohol please?" Mark whispered in a horrified voice to David.

"Why? Are you ashamed of me?"

Mel quickly moved on, smirking at Mark's discomfort.

The cool night air was a welcome relief, after being inside with so many people. For a moment they were silent enjoying the stillness and relative quiet.

"So... What can I help you with?" Mel asked putting her best business face on.

He smiled down at her.

"Nothing I just really wanted to get you alone."

Chapter 4

"Really, and why is that?" she asked, still smiling up at him.

Mel felt a small thrill, as she walked slowly towards him on the small balcony.

"I'm interested in your line of work," he said, smiling back.

Mel raised an eyebrow.

"Insurance? Seriously? That's got to be the worst pick up line anyone has ever used on me," Mel laughed at his awkwardness.

"Okay, you got me." He grinned back at her, "I'm not interested in insurance. By the way, I'm Nick."

He looked mischievous, but there was something darker was swimming in his expression.

"Then what are you interested in?" Mel asked, softly looking up into his eyes then lowering her eyes to look at his lips.

Suddenly Nick took a step back, looking at Mel for a moment.

Cold amusement slipped into his expression.

"You know you have a good job, and good friends. I really don't understand why you need to do this to yourself."

"Do what?" Mel asked, baffled at his sudden change.

"You know. All of this," He gestured back to the bedroom, and living room inside.

"Oh. Shit." Mel stuttered in shock. "You think I was selling my body for insurance clients?"

Mel's heart faltered, then started to race in a bad way, she couldn't be any more mortified, could her life get any worse?

He stared at Mel for a moment, looking almost as shocked as she was, then he began to speak quickly.

"No. No. I didn't mean that."

"Oh, thank God for that," Mel allowed a small smile, relieved and her heart rate lowered slightly.

"I meant, how you rip off people's bank accounts on the Internet."

"WHAT?!! You're not from The Shed? That was you? Seriously did you not read my emails? IT'S NOT ME!" Her reaction was instant and loud.

Mel was stunned.

As cute as he was, this man was obviously a deranged psycho, *and in her home, at her party!*

"Yeah right," he drawled, as his gaze on her turned wintry. "And what I'm wondering is, why are you throwing a party, when your life should be in the toilet by now."

Looking up at him now, Mel began to feel her initial attraction to him morph into something else entirely. Her heart was still racing as she felt her temper slip out of her control.

Resisting the urge to start slapping him was hard work, so Mel tried to concentrate on making her words slow and even, as she spoke.

"Are you always this stupid, or are you just making a special effort today? **You self-righteous, sanctimonious, asshole!** How dare you invade my life like this! What the hell did I ever do to you? You are one sick fuck, you know that! You have systematically ruined my life."

Mel started off slow but soon words tumbled out, and she was screeching at him. Only stopping when she ran out of breath.

"Do you have *any* idea what I have been through because of you?"

"Um. Yes. That's why I did it." Nick said, looking as if someone really had slapped him. "Are you saying you didn't take my money?"

"Dip-shit! *I Have Not Got Your Money!* You've got mine remember?"

When it came to temper control, counting to ten only gave Mel more time to think up worse things to say, so she never bothered.

Mel suddenly remembered all the things she had thought of, for when this time came.

"I'm sure your parents must be so proud of having such a vindictive, cruel, person like you for a son," Mel said slowly, turning the volume down to a quiet snarl.

"Um," Nick backed off a step, looking distinctly rattled.

"You know what the worst part about you is? I bet you're the type of person that thinks he's still a good guy underneath it all. You think that sure you've done a couple of bad things, but you think overall you're still a nice person, right?"

Mel's eyes had narrowed dangerously. "The fact of the matter is, that you're the type of scum who makes this world a worse place for being in it. You are not a diamond in the rough, or misunderstood. You're simply a sadistic moron. Hell bent on getting your own way, no matter who you have to hurt."

Nick swayed slightly and took another step back, and was looking glassy eyed from the verbal onslaught.

"Look, if you didn't do it then who did?" He asked when he could get a word in.

"I don't know. You pathetic ass wipe. If I did, I would have emailed you with their details. Just like I emailed before, remember? When I was telling you that I wasn't doing anything to you!"

Mel was beginning to run out of breath again and steam.

Her temper always happened like that. If she let her temper out quickly and safely, it didn't get bottled up and become worse.

"I've only been hooked up to the Internet for six months now, and I was a novice before then."

"If you've only been on-line for six months, you still

are a novice," Nick said.

"Pardon?" Mel snarked. "Did you seriously just insult me?"

She gripped her glass tightly, so she wouldn't be tempted to throw it at his smug face.

"How much was you last Internet bill?" Nick asked quickly. He was looking thoughtful, and nervously, at Mel.

"Huh? What does that have to do with anything?"

"Well, someone close by, could be hacking your Wi-Fi," Nick paused thinking quickly. "That's how I would do it if I was worried about being caught. Did the bill add up, or was it over what you thought your usage should be?"

"How the hell am I supposed to work out what my usage should be, if I've never been on-line before?" Calming down she tried to use a more moderate tone of voice as she kicked her brain into high gear. "Does this mean you finally believe me now?"

"Ah… um… I'm open to the possibility."

"What?!" Mel ground out. "You know if you were twice as smart, you'd still be stupid."

"Okay. Fine, I believe you."

Nick had always hated admitting when he was wrong, and this was no exception. But he was having trouble believing that Mel was anything but a novice in the computer world.

To start with she had far too active a social life, and she had none of the necessary gear either in her lounge or bedroom that he had snooped though earlier.

"You better had." Mel looked around.

Everyone inside was staring at them though the glass doors.

Mel's parties, despite the dancing, alcohol and sly hook ups, were usually civil affairs. Anyone else would have been thrown out for yelling.

As it was Mel's apartment everyone took another second to stare as Mel looked back at them. Narrowing her eyes at the party guests, they quickly got the message and went back to their conversations, keeping their eyes averted from the balcony.

"You can leave now," Mel said stiffly to Nick.

"Sure." Nick waited for a beat. "But I want to find out who has been using you as cover. Can I come back tomorrow?"

"11am and don't be late. You have some serious explaining to do."

Mel turned on her heel, and went back to the door of the balcony towards her guests.

"Right now, you can get the hell out." She held the balcony door open for him to leave.

Nick noticed that a few people had already discreetly slipped out, and after looking at the expression on Mel's face he decided to follow suit without comment.

Two minutes after Nick had left, Mel realized she didn't get his last name, or any other details, so that she could contact him and pay him back by making his life a living hell.

The party ended sooner than usual at 2 am. When the last person had left, Mel realized that she had forgotten to record any drunkenness from later in the party and only had her cell phone recordings of her boss's boyfriend dancing on the coffee table to fall back on.

Crap.

Oh well.

At least one person was going to be nice to her this week, unless he wanted the footage uploaded to face-book.

Not that much had happened; it seemed that the main entertainment for the night had been her little spat with the '*Suck It*' man. Really table dancing was kind of tame anyway.

Mel realized she had no choice now, but to be nice to the jerk tomorrow, and hope he gave her all her money back. Mark and David were the last to leave. David had taken Mark's comments about not drinking to heart, and proceeded to get completely smashed.

Mark surprised Mel again that night, by easily lifting David up with a fireman's hold, to carry him out to the waiting taxi.

At 11am the next morning Nick arrived looking bright, alert, clean shaven and contrite.

Mel felt hung over and sleep deprived, as she opened the door to him.

Looking up to him, she had to quickly hold her breath, and she suppressed the urge to flirt with him. Here was the guy who had recently confessed to making the last two weeks a living hell, and she wanted to flirt?

Maybe she had been hit with the stupid stick when she was younger.

Being cute wasn't going to get Mel any of her money back. The apartment had been trashed the night before, and she hadn't had time to set the apartment back to order yet.

Wine glasses, bottles and food plates lay on the kitchen bench and party streamers littered the floor.

"So what do you want me to call you, Mr Techy Tubby? I'm not yelling 'Hey Suck It,' in a crowded room," Mel slung at him as soon as he had walked inside.

"My name is Nickolas Mann, you can call me Nick," he stated coolly. "Like I told you last night."

"Like I care!" Mel was getting more steamed by the second.

The fact that she wanted to go for a roll in the hay with Nick, only made her angrier. "Do you know what you've done to me? I had to get on the bus with smelly people every day to work, at I job I hate, that I wasn't even going to get paid for! My boss thinks I'm nuts, and I have debt collectors chasing me and I can't even make a phone call to my friends, or buy so much as a chocolate bar!"

"Look I know I went a bit far," Nick said, trying to

remain calm. "But seriously, how was I to know? I thought you'd be some short fat geek looking to make a quick buck, not an innocent inept bystander."

"Did you just call me inept?" Mel's voice suddenly got dangerously quiet, as her eyes narrowed.

"Ah. No, that's not what I meant," Nick paused, trying his best not to show that he was panicking internally, but failing.

"How did you know about the party last night?" Mel asked after a tense moment.

"I've been watching your e-mails, and thought that it would the best way to slip in and out without you noticing."

There was a knock at the door, and with a quick glare at Nick, Mel stalked over and opened it, and looked down towards a disgruntled Max, from the next door apartment.

Looking as unkempt as always, Max gave off his usual odor of cheese balls and desperation.

"Could you two lovebirds keep it down, I'm trying to work," Max glared up at Mel. "The party last night was bad enough, but you could at least keep it down during the day."

Max glanced at Nick, and stared for a moment, realizing he had just potentially insulted a man nearly a foot taller than himself, before quickly waddling back to his own apartment.

"Great now you've got my neighbor complaining," Mel snarled at Nick.

Nick didn't respond, as he was still looking at the closed door with a frozen face.

"Nick. Hello! You were in the middle of saying sorry to me for ruining my life."

"How close do you think his apartment is from yours?" Nick asked quietly, looking thoughtful.

"It's right next door. Why?" Mel asked slightly put out at the conversation change.

"Because he is *exactly* the stereotype I thought of when

my accountant was broken into, and this first started out." Nick paused. "And because someone is using your Wi-Fi to do all this, so it has to be within a certain range of your connection."

"You're going to need to explain that sentence," Mel said poker-faced, "I don't speak geek. Also, you shouldn't stereotype people so much."

"My accountant was broken into around six months ago, and my credit card details, along with several other people's information was stolen. It happened on a Friday night, and the accountant didn't notice till after the long weekend on Tuesday morning. By the time the police realized what had happened, and I was notified, the hacker had maxed out all of my cards." Nick did his best to explain the situation to Mel, he had made the worst possible first impression, and he really wanted to fix things with her.

"I did my best to trace the money, but the hacker had set up bogus websites and then transferred the money offshore into bank accounts, in both Taiwan and Switzerland. In short, I can't touch the person doing it and I can't get back my money." He drew a breath, obviously still angry.

"How much did he take from you?" Mel was curious.

"None of your business." Nick turned back to look at the computer lying on the coffee table then back to Mel. "Is there anyone else on this floor?"

"Nope, it's two apartments per floor." Mel calmed down again. "Do you think it's him?"

"Yes, if I'm wrong, I'll apologize in person to him, though I need to see who's using and doing what on your connection, to be sure. Look, I understand that I was cruel to you. If you don't want me to the things that I did to you, I will understand. But I need to get Max to stop what he's doing," Nick pleaded.

"Are you saying you'll go easy on him?" Mel was

stunned. After all Nick had done to her! Now he was going to go easy on the tubby rat! "I mean if it is Max that's doing this."

"If that's what you want. I will." Nick moved in closer looking down into her eyes.

"Wow, you really don't know me that well." Mel gave him an evil grin, and Nick felt a small thrill go through him. "We are going to have some fun with this little turd. Straight after you fix my money, and cell problems. Then you can get to hacking into whoever is using my computer, I mean my Wi-Fi."

"Really?" Nick asked. "What happened to me being an evil sadist, and all that?"

"What can I say? I'm not that nice a person either, and I don't mind so much if it's not happening to me." Mel waited for a moment. "The difference between you and me. is that I know that I'm mean and nasty as hell, and I'm quite OK with it."

Nick stared down at her in surprise.

"Remind me not to piss you off,"

"Way too late for that buster, and I need my money back."

Looking around the room, Nick saw scrotum shriveling pastel colors and womanly, homey touches all around him.

Repressing an urge to shudder, he sat down to Mel's laptop and got to work. When Mel finished making coffee, and a plate of leftover snacks from the party, she found Nick hard at work correcting and replacing all her money. Together they first put all of Mel's credit cards, and phone accounts to rights. It would take a day to show up in Mel's accounts, but the money should be in her accounts after that. Then they went to work on investigating the person who was piggy backing Mel's account.

It was impressive watching Nick work, Mel had to admit, but when she asked him how he knew how to do all of this he clammed up for several minutes, and Mel got the message. After the first hour or so they both began to loosen up a bit, and to tentatively joke around with each other.

"You haven't been playing on-line role playing games?" Nick smiled at the computer as he asked.

"Huh? What are they?" Mel asked "Is that like the Dungeons and Dragons stuff the losers play?"

"I'll take that as a no, then." Nick said still smiling. "Also on-line gaming is a lot more sophisticated than the old days of board games of D&D."

Mel snorted, "Anything you can play in your underwear, alone, while eating, is not sophisticated. No matter how cool the geeks think it is."

Nick opened his mouth to argue back, but realized he really couldn't fault those points, so he closed his mouth and got back to sorting out the two different personalities who had been logging on under the same name.

Really it was quite easy, Mel shopped for shoes and dresses, and the hacker gamed a little on Mel's account and moved money around. Their personalities were very different.

"So, how did you get around me changing my passwords all the time?" Mel was curious about a lot of things, but self-defense was always first, and if she could prevent this from happening again then she should.

"When I thought you might have stolen my money, I installed a key counter virus on your computer, and then figured out your credit card number, passwords and personal details. It did throw me when you did stuff from your work computer, but then you checked your balance at home, and I could get in again."

"Huh." Mel thought for a moment. "And how do I stop it from happening again?"

Nick looked up for a moment. "I'll install a firewall and some virus protection, as soon as we have figured out who was stealing my money. If we do it now it will give Max a heads up something is wrong."

"Okay." Mel hadn't felt so inept in a long time. "Are you sure it's him yet? Max, I mean."

"Not yet. But below you within range of your Wi Fi are: An elderly woman who doesn't own a computer, and above you are two single men who work in construction."

"Engineers?"

"No, they work as general laborers. They have no computing experience, and mostly they surf porn." Nick grinned. "It really looks like Max is the only candidate. I do want to make sure it is him, and not a visitor or relative who visits regularly though."

"So, what now then?" Mel asked.

"I go home, and check Max out from my computer."

"Why not do it now?" Mel asked impatiently.

"From the same I.P. address as he is using?" Nick looked at Mel like she was stupid. "No, that would let him know that I was onto him."

"Fine. Let's talk about what we are going to do when we find out for sure it is him."

They agreed on a plan of attack that involved three simple steps, first, torture Max. Second ask him to confess to his crimes wait for him to refuse, and finally torture him again until he went to the police and handed himself in.

Mel loved the simplicity of it.

Things seemed to get tense between them when it was time for Nick to say goodbye, Mel realized that the morning meeting with Nick had lead into afternoon.

They were laughing sometimes, and the day had now assumed a 'date' like atmosphere. When Nick paused outside the door he smiled down at Mel, with his big brown eyes, as Mel stared back up at him for a moment.

Then she swung the door shut in his face, with a satisfying thud.

After a moment she quickly re-opened it, smiled at Nick and then got her jacket and purse from the counter, and held out her hand.

She smiled up at him.

"I need at least two hundred dollars, so I can go shopping for food. I'm out of everything."

Chapter 5

Mel woke Monday morning feeling tired, having been up all day, and part of Sunday night, cleaning up from the party. Not to mention the last few weeks of sloppiness.

Catching a taxi to work felt like a long lost luxury, after two weeks of living on a financial knife edge.

At work Mel sighed as she sat in her cubical, and kept trying to think about what Max had done, and trying to think up what to do to Max, but instead she kept thinking about how hot Nick was.

It seemed fairly obvious that Max was the culprit, but she would wait to make sure. She would not be some idiot that went off without knowing for sure, like Nick had been.

She wanted a little revenge on Nick, for all the trouble he had caused her, but Mel wanted far more trouble for Max, as he was the underlying cause of all the problems.

Nick was only trying to get his money back as far as Mel could see, where as Max had deliberately stolen Nick's money, and used her Internet connection to do it.

Several things that she had in mind originally for *'Suck It'* could be swapped over to Max, just in case Max didn't want to hand himself over to the police straight away. Mel knew she had to have a plan ready for both Max and Nick.

Mel also spent a while thinking about how Nick must have felt when he realized that someone had stolen his money from his credit cards. Although stealing from Mel didn't make things right, she could see where he had been coming from.

Calling Sal, and arranging to meet her and Di for coffee at their favorite cafe around lunch time, was the only constructive thing Mel could think of before lunch. The footage of David at her party had already come in handy when Mark had started to frown at Mel's request for a longer lunch than usual.

She visited a money machine on the way, and withdrew the money she owed to Di and Sal.

Then she bought enough candy to restock the chocolate stash at the back of the top cupboard.

The stash Regina bought her had been hit hard.

An hour later the three friends met at the cafe and were enjoying coffee, sandwiches and cake, Mel's treat of course.

"Are you sure it's your neighbor Max?" Di asked, after Mel had explained the situation at length to them.

"Not really, but Nick is," Mel replied sipping her coffee. It tasted like cinnamon and freedom. "He's checking to make sure it's not a friend who visits regularly or anything, but Nick seems pretty sure."

"And how do you know this isn't some new ploy to mess up your life in new and interesting ways again?" asked Sal, the optimist.

"Because I spent several hours with him yesterday, and frankly he doesn't seem to have it in him." Mel said calmly, smiling. "I think he has little a crush on me."

Sal and Di looked stunned.

"You like him!" They said in unison.

Mel grinned and shrugged, not bothering to deny it.

"Maybe, but I wouldn't trust him as far as I could throw him, and he is beginning to trust me, which is stupid of him."

"What are you going to do to him?" Di asked.

Di and Sal were well versed in Mel's long history of pissed off temper tantrums.

"To Nick or Max?" Mel asked. "Truthfully, I don't know just yet. I've got a few ideas, but I was kind of hoping you two could give me some inspiration."

Sal and Di smiled at each other.

"Well, as I work for a chemist, I can offer a number of

solutions." Sal said.

"True, I didn't think of that route. Should I buy the drink that makes your urine red or blue?" Mel wondered out loud.

"Red that way he might go to a doctor, and they would have to do a lot of invasive exams to figure out that there is nothing wrong," Di offered.

"Also any lubricant you find at his house would have to be replaced with deep heat," Sal added, warming to the subject.

"Ick. No. That would mean going into his apartment and touching…"

Mel stopped her train of thought right there. "Nope, I think that would be more horrible for me, than for him."

"What about giving him symptoms of half a dozen different diseases?" Di suggested. "Psychological warfare, and all."

"Laxative brownies, red dye in his drinks and itching powder in his washing, all at the same time will make for an interesting doctors visit," Mel mused.

"You could also go down the ex- girlfriend route, and find out what family he has," Sal suggested.

"Oh, good one."

Mel was always grateful for her friends help, and although she had already thought of the ex-girlfriend idea she didn't want to stem the creative flow.

"I have some good footage from that work party at my place the other night. Mark's partner David got loud and obnoxious, tried to table surf and fell off. Other than that nothing much else happened. I got the table surfing parts on my phone. If you want to come over and we can watch it on the big screen."

Mel loved that her friends hated the snobbery at her day job, and before they all went their separate ways, they organized another girl's night at Mel's place with cheesy movies and food.

It was the perfect way for Mel to thank them for all their help in the past few weeks.

Mel remembered to pay them back all money she owed them before they left.

After the work day had finished she stopped at the chemist where Sal worked, Mel bought the list of recommended products and accessories and was unpacking them when her cell-phone rang.

Mel had arrived home that evening in a much better mood and thanks to her friends, she had an excellent plan of attack for both Nick and Max.

"Can I come over and check a few things out from your end?" Nick asked. "I still want to make certain that it's Max before I start hacking again. I don't want another slip up."

"Sure," Mel replied. "But I don't remember giving you this number."

"I emptied your bank account, maxed out your credit cards, froze your phone account, and that's your question?"

Nick laughed at her.

"I said you could come over, but don't you start mocking me, or it will go very badly for you," Mel said looking at her bag full of equipment.

"I'll see you in an hour or so."

He was still laughing at her as he hung up.

After Mel had packed the supplies away she wrote a quick list of what to use on who and when.

Then she checked the orange juice and realized there was only a glass left in the bottle and quickly poured some of the red dye in.

Really Nick shouldn't be so rude, she was only trying to help him.

Tiding up the apartment again, she got a second load of washing ready by the door as Nick arrived.

"About time, I have stuff to do," Mel said, by way of

greeting when she opened the door to him.

"What are you going to do?" Nick asked, still looking amused as he walked in, then he saw the washing pile. "Are you going to trust me in your apartment alone? After everything I did?"

"Well, Max is doing his washing downstairs at the moment. I saw he had used up all three machines, when I went to do mine just before. So I'll start with adding itching powder to his washing and work my way up." Mel said. "You can work on figuring out if it is really him, with some actual evidence rather than living in the right place."

Mel wasn't too worried if it turned out that Max wasn't the culprit, there was no way itching powder had any way of coming back to her.

She grinned to herself as she walked to the door. "There's orange juice on the counter, and help yourself to food."

Nick shook his head at Mel, as she left with her washing basket.

Arriving back a few minutes later, Mel found Nick working on the computer at her coffee table with an empty glass beside him, and the empty juice container on the bench.

"It's defiantly him," Nick stated. "He games a little bit on your account, then remembers to change back to his own, so your bill isn't too high."

Smiling to herself, Mel decided to let Nick get on with things while she wrote down a quick schedule of attack. After an hour of quietly working on his laptop, Nick announced he had finished for the day, and abruptly left. The wanting look on Nick's face as he left, was a pleasant surprise for Mel.

Nick obviously liked her and didn't have a clue what to do about it.

She looked at the closing door in puzzlement and then shook her head. Well, maybe she could help him out with that problem too. Mel wondered if he had been trying to make small talk for the past hour and she hadn't picked up on it.

Mel smiled as she imagined teasing Nick about his crush on her.

When Regina arrived at Mel's apartment only minutes after Nick had left, she found Mel looking more alive than she had for weeks.

"You're looking brighter." Regina remarked as she walked in with Chinese takeout in her arms. She looked around the apartment. "This place is looking cleaner than it has for a while."

"Yup. Guess who gate crashed my party?" Mel smirked.

"No! The nerve of that bastard. Did you get a name and address?" Regina's eyes narrowed. "Was it man or woman? What did they look like?"

"His name is Nick, and he's not necessarily a bad guy." Mel said to Regina's astonishment. "He is an idiot, but he's not the only idiot I have to deal with."

"Explain." Regina spoke crisply.

"Well… he has been ripped off by someone, and he thought it was me, so he tried to get revenge for the money he lost. He realized that I'm not the culprit and he has returned my money. He's working on getting my cell back on and then we are both going to find out who really ripped him off."

"And you are just letting him off the hook?" Regina was aghast. "Just like that? He says 'Oops, sorry.' And it's all fine with you?"

"Don't be ridiculous, of course not."

Mel investigated the takeaway bags and then pulled out a few plates and forks, ignoring the chop sticks.

"I'm just going to dial it back a little, and save some ideas for the real culprit of all this misery."

The two women spent the rest of the evening assigning different ideas for revenge to Nick and Max.

The next Monday evening, Max was collecting his post from the downstairs lobby when Mel arrived home from work.

"Hi." Mel smiled at him, as she stopped to check her letterbox too.

"Um. Hi?" Max looked up in surprise.

Women didn't usually pay Max much attention, and up until recently Mel had barely nodded to him. Max was confident in his position in the shallow end of the gene pool.

Mel had started the day with the theory that if someone was a thief, and okay with it, then they weren't too picky about where their things came from. So she had thought of a simple, yet effective, first attack on Max.

"Gosh, someone's forgotten their groceries," Mel commented on the single abandoned supermarket bag beside the post box.

"What?" Max looked down and saw the orange juice, toilet paper and other essentials sticking out.

"Oh no… Um that's mine. I just put it down to get the mail," Max stuttered scooping the bag up quickly.

"Oh." Mel gave him a small smile, "Okay bye,"

She turned to walk away before smiling broadly to herself.

Mel had wondered if taking money over the Internet was going to make Max more inclined to stealing if there was no one around to see.

She was glad she had taken the time to tamper with all of the groceries before carefully repacking them.

Dinner with Regina was a fun affair that night, Mel made the feta and spinach pizza again. Then she told Regina about the letterbox affair, Regina laughed and laughed.

On Friday morning as she was leaving for work, Mel saw Max standing outside his apartment, looking slightly worse for wear. Grey faced and tired he was heading out as well. Walking out her door she quickly plastered on a fake smile.

"Hi Max, how are you?"

"Oh. Hi, Mel." Max squirmed for a moment. "I'm good, I've just got a touch of the stomach flu."

"Oh, you poor thing," Mel said sympathetically, "Wait here a moment."

Mel quickly went back to her apartment, and brought back a small box of her home-made brownies. She handed them over to a baffled Max with a small smile. She walked to the taxi stand with a smile on her face that lasted nearly all day. Revenge was such a sweet dish.

Saturday morning, Mel had arranged to meet with Nick again. She looked up from the computer, as soon as the knock hit the door. Nick entered the apartment quickly.

"So how are the pranks going?"

Nick asked as soon as he had walked in. His hair looked like he had deliberately ruffled and styled, as he walked into the lounge and over to the laptop that Mel had set up at the lounge couch, with her feet up and a coffee beside her.

"Pranks?" Mel queried noticing his hair as she looked up briefly. "You don't seem to respect what I'm bringing to this little revenge party of yours."

"I didn't mean that I don't respect you, but you have to admit that itching power doesn't really stack up against having all your credit cards declined at once," Nick said not understanding how condescending he sounded.

"No," said Mel sweetly. "But this morning Max went to two different doctors to be probed and prodded in all his fun places because he hasn't realized that I slipped a red dye into his orange juice the other day and that's making him pee red."

Nick stood still for a moment, jaw slack, staring at Mel.

"I talked to him in the hall again. I know that you had to go to the doctor too, but after what you did to me I thought you needed a bit of payback," Mel said, still smiling sweetly at Nick. "I think we can say we're even now. But seriously don't try any of your crap on me again or I may call your Mum and tell her what you did to me."

Mel smiled and remembered all the annoying small talk she had to make with Nick the other day, before he opened up to her about his mother. Nick's face turned red first, then gray, then gradually turned back to normal again as he fought against several different emotions.

Not in the least of which, she suspected, was walking out and never coming back.

Mel watched Nick with interest, as he slowly regained his temper.

"Can you do worse to Max?" He eventually asked. Revenge was why Nick was here, and the fact was, if Mel could do what she had done to Nick this morning, then she had to have worse in store for Max.

Mel looked up into his warm eyes and nearly forgot what she had been talking about. Fortunately her mouth was still running on automatic.

"Of course I can." Mel said turning back to her computer quickly to cover her discomfort.

"I have already, he's been to two doctors already."

Nick saw she was watching a live feed of Max standing outside his apartment, on the computer, as he scratched himself and looked for his keys.

Nick had installed a tiny camera outside her apartment last week, so she could watch the corridor.

The itching power and red dye had proved to be a serious problem for Max. The main problem seemed to be in the anal area, Mel had to laugh when she remembered him squirming in the hallway, while he was talking to her.

"Why is it so much worse for him?" Asked Nick, as he

thought about when Mel had slipped the red dye into his drink.

"Possibly it is psychological, because of the red pee, but I think it is mainly caused by the itching power that I put in his toilet paper. It took forever to unroll, sprinkle and then re-roll it back up after, but I think the effect was worth it don't you? He has another weeks' worth of it to get through."

Nick watched the computer monitor and admired Mel's handy work. Mel's expression seemed to have gone from wide-eyed innocence, to evil psycho in a split second, when Nick looked back to her.

"When we tell him to go to the police, and give him a warning about what will happen if he doesn't go. Then I can tell him what I've already done, let Max figure out what you did and then change tactics to something else."

Nick was looking at her with an odd expression on his face, as several different emotions again fought for dominance. Nick was unsure whether he should be impressed, afraid or seriously turned on by Mel. This woman was obviously nuts, but in a really fun way.

"What will you do then?" he finally asked, half afraid of the answer.

Mel grinned and looked back at the laptop and picked up her coffee.

"Don't worry, I've got it covered," she said. "Help yourself to a coffee and food if you get hungry."

Nick gave Mel a sour look. Mel kept smiling, and turned back to her drink.

After a few minutes, Nick was sure Mel was concentrating on her computer resending all her missed payments. So Nick carefully ate a small section of brownie that had crumbled off. With all the stress Mel had put him under lately, he could use all the help he could get.

"I passed Max in the hall yesterday and he said he wasn't feeling well, so I thought I could spare him a few of my batch of homemade brownies."

Nick looked at the kitchen counter that showed baking utensils and flour littered along it along, with a box of chocolate laxative chews and a bottle of 'Quick & Fast'.

"You are giving him the runs, as well as all the other stuff? Impressive."

"Yup, I believe it is called psychological warfare." Mel glanced over at the kitchen following Nick's gaze. Turning back to the computer, Mel offered the computer to Nick while she got up to make a pot of coffee.

The two of them had stayed up late the previous night, hacking into Max's life and making small talk while Nick hacked and slashed through Max's firewalls. They were now completely certain he had stolen Nick's money in his accounts, along with several other people's money.

They disagreed with what to do with all the other victim's money, but eventually common sense prevailed, and they decided that Nick would leave it in a place that the techs at the police station could easily track and retrieve it.

Two weeks later, Mel's spying had shown her that Max had suffered through a week's worth of missing money, itchiness and invasive doctor's procedures.

He had plenty of bills now racked up and his credit card company had now looked into hiring a debt recovery agent. But this didn't mean Max was going to be ready to give himself up when he was confronted. Also he didn't know what the hell was going on just yet.

Nick had made his plans for the next step, so Mel felt she needed to as well.

After thinking of all the things she could do, in the end Mel felt the only option that was even vaguely appropriate for Max, was the wounded ex-girlfriend routine. So, early that morning she went shopping at the prenatal section of the clothing shops, in the mall, and bought the appropriate equipment for the job.

Mel had agreed to meet Nick at ten in the morning at a coffee shop. It was getting close to that time before she had made her purchases. Hurrying to the cafe was so undignified, but Mel was still eager to see Nick again. Slowing down she had to ask herself why?

It wasn't like she cared what he thought of her punctuality. Or was there something else going on that she didn't want to admit to?

Mel knew that Nick was her type, but perhaps there was more to it than a basic attraction.

They had seen a disturbing amount of each other in the past week and Mel was sure he was beginning to make up excuses to come over. Nick hadn't needed to be within a certain range to hack Max's accounts had he? She had no idea.

Finding a partner for the night was never much of a challenge, with Mel's confidence. But this felt different to her.

Shaking off the distracting thoughts of Nick naked in bed, Mel saw him sitting at the cafe waiting patiently for her. Nick had already been served his hot chocolate.

"Nice of you to join me. I was beginning to think I was going to be drinking alone today." Nick smiled up at her, his eyes twinkling.

"Sorry, I got caught up shopping for our mutual friend." Mel said smiling back, then cursed herself for her reaction.

"Me too." Nick showed her the surveillance equipment he had bought, nicely packaged up and in plastic bags beside his feet.

"Nice, but how are you going to get it in there?" Mel asked nodding at the small video cameras and microphones.

"Yeah, I need a distraction because this really is a two person job." Nick made puppy dog eyes at Mel. "Please help? Just find a way to get him out for around 20 minutes. And I'll need to have access to your place to check it works."

"Sure thing, I'll ask him out for coffee." Mel smiled back at Nick, and made a mental note to check her own apartment for any bugs and cameras that Nick may have installed after her 'coffee' with Max.

"I love how women can do that," Nick sighed.

"What?" Mel asked in surprise.

"Just snap their fingers, and men go out with them," Nick said with a scowl on his face.

Mel said nothing as her coffee was served, and just smiled at him.

"This will be a perfect time to confront him, and try to get him to come clean to the police." Mel said after her first careful sip.

"Nope, you can't do that," Nick said firmly.

"Why not?" Mel asked sweetly, knowing exactly why Nick didn't want her going out with Max. He would never admit he was jealous.

Nick paused, not wanting to admit why he hated the idea so much, the gears in his head spun quickly trying to figure out how he could talk her out of it.

"Because I want to see the expression on his smug little face when he realizes what I've been doing to him," Nick managed finally.

"Fine. I'll ask him out for coffee, and chat with him for a while and you can come when you've finished bugging his apartment. That way if he tries to leave early, I can text you to give you a heads up. Also, I get to manipulate him some more before you arrive." Mel replied.

"Okay. When do you want to do that?"

"Um… give him a week. With his current symptoms it will take that long for the labs to come back clear," Mel said.

"What lab tests?" Nick asked surprised.

"Oh, the itching powder I put in his washing have caused a massive rash all over his body." Mel looked at Nick puzzled. "Along with the laxative brownies and more itching powder in his toilet paper?"

"Yes, so?"

"So he's had to go in for some nasty tests, and right now he's freaking that he has some horrible disease and I want him to suffer with that thought, for as long as possible."

Nick smiled at Mel with more respect in his eyes than he had a few weeks ago. He finished his hot chocolate, and turned to leave.

"I'll see you in a few days."

"Why? We can see each other next week when we talk to Max."

"No, I'll need to hack his computer and it will be easier if I can do it from within his own Wi-Fi."

Nick looked surprised at Mel's lack of basic computer knowledge.

"You mean my Wi-Fi. Fine. Text me and we can arrange a time," Mel said drinking her coffee slowly, and thinking about how Nick's attitude towards her was changing. He seemed to be getting a healthy respect for her 'old school' methods of revenge.

"Bye," Nick looked like he wanted to hang around but didn't really know how to say it.

"Don't let the door hit you on the way out credit killer," Mel smiled at him. Nick grinned awkwardly and left.

Chapter 6

Saturday morning a week later, Max was coming out of his apartment when, coincidently, Mel also walked out of her apartment, with her arm around her washing basket.

Mel had the door partly open all morning, with the basket beside it, waiting for him to surface.

"Hi, Max."

Mel had made sure to wear a low cut t-shirt, that showed her limited assets to the best of her ability. Skinny jeans to show off her legs, and a chunky belt to disguise the middle spread. With her understated makeup, Mel knew she looked just like the sexy, hot girl next door.

The natural look, ironically, always took over an hour to achieve.

"Did you like the brownies I gave you?"

He looked slightly puzzled at all the niceness that Mel had been showing him lately.

Max smelled of fried bacon grease today, and looked as clean as he usually did, which was not very. "Laundry day, huh?" He nodded at the basket.

"Yup, what about you?" Mel smiled and shifted her washing basket so that her hip popped out a little more.

"Oh, I was just..." Max looked around franticly. The ball had finally dropped, and Max realized he might actually have a chance with Mel, and he wondered why it had taken him so long to figure it out.

"I was just getting mine, too."

Mel smiled at him. "I'll see you down there soon,"

"Sure."

Max stood outside his apartment for a moment, slightly stunned at the turn of the conversation. He watched Mel as she walked away, then seemed to shake himself and raced back to his apartment for his washing.

Less than two minutes later, Max was walking slowly

through the shared laundry room door, looking slightly sweaty, and trying not to puff.

"Hi, again." Max squeaked out at her.

"Hi, Max," Mel smiled looking down at him, and straight into his eyes. Trying not to notice how badly he needed a facial ex-foliation. "How's your day going?"

Mel had nearly finished putting her clothes in the machines, and was watching Max with concealed amusement.

"Great, thanks." Max had stopped in the middle of the room, and was staring at Mel like a dog looking into a butcher's shop window.

"Did you have some laundry to do?" Mel reminded him gently.

"Huh? Oh yes." Max glanced at the clothes in his hands, and quickly turned to face one of the machines. Mel turned back to her machine, and rolled her eyes. Quickly finishing her task, Mel waited for Max to finish stuffing all his clothes into one machine and turn it on.

Max stared at the buttons for a moment before Mel spoke again.

"Just press start, after you've put your coins in," she offered helpfully.

"Oh, right," Max quickly searched his pockets. "I have lots of money you know. Just not here this minute."

"Would you like to borrow a few coins?" Mel's smile was genuine now. It was nice to know she still had it, even if she didn't always use it.

"Uh, yes please," Max stammered. "Sorry, I don't usually do this."

"Do what? Your laundry?" Mel asked, trying to sound like she was joking.

"No, I mean my Mum usually helps… look can I ask you out for dinner?" Max realized he may be beginning to lose his cool image a little, so hurried to his main objective.

"Not as a date or anything, but just for helping with the

machine. Not that I wouldn't ask you out… I've got lots of money. Let me pay you back."

"A coffee would be fine, Max," Mel had to interrupt, or she would crack up laughing. "Also, I have no problem with close families. It's something the world could use more of."

Max's smile of shock, and relief said it all.

"Great. How about at the cafe' down the road? We could go now?" Max said, thinking he was pressing his advantage.

"Sure. Oh, um. Can you give me an hour to finish the housework first? I was kind of in the middle of it all, and I hate leaving things a mess," Mel quickly amended. She wasn't sure if Nick could get to Max's apartment that fast.

"Okay, I'll see you in an hour."

"Bye, Max."

Mel's face was beginning to hurt from smiling so much. Walking back upstairs to her apartment, Mel dropped the smile and shut the door firmly behind her, then she quickly called Nick.

"You are on for the cameras, and tech stuff in one hour," Mel informed him.

"You had better be able to do it now, because I'm not going out with this dork twice."

"I'll be there, just keep him at the coffee shop till I'm done, and I turn up to talk to him."

"Unfortunately, that won't be a problem."

Mel hung up, then looked around at her apartment quickly to make sure everything was in order, and to make sure there were no little hiding places for cameras or bugs of any kind.

Although things had been going well with Nick, she still wasn't sure how much she trusted him.

Then she put her feet up and watched T.V. for a while until it was time to go.

Getting her coat, Mel opened her door to Max, who was

obviously just about to knock.

Max had changed in to clothes that were slightly less stained, and smelled slightly more like pizza than bacon. The overall effect was more of a change than an improvement though.

"Are you ready to go?" He asked, bouncing slightly from one foot to the other.

"Sure thing," Mel replied, putting her smile firmly back in place and trying to make as much eye contact as she could bear.

Walking down to the cafe, they talked about Max's mother and how she usually came over and did all his laundry with him, but how Max liked the independence of living alone, which was why he had gotten his own place last year despite being only thirty years old.

Mel nodded, and waited for a lull in the talking before asking more probing questions. She was feeling as though her face was starting to freeze up from smiling so much.

At the cafe, Max seemed to realize that he was doing all the talking.

"So did you get all the housework done?"

He asked after they had been seated and the coffee had arrived.

"Oh, yes but I didn't wipe down the windows. I might leave that for next weekend," Mel said lightly.

"Wow. You do windows?" This was obviously a new concept for Max. "I did tidy up my place a bit though, in case you wanted to come back after?"

Mel choked on her coffee slightly, and quickly repressed a shudder.

"Let's just have coffee first and see."

Where the hell was Nick? Mel gave in and checked her phone for texts, Max didn't seem to mind her poor phone etiquette.

Perhaps he was used to people only half paying attention to him, Mel thought.

Ten minutes to go. Sorry.

Damn it, she had only been here half an hour, and Mel was already getting desperate to leave.

She could only be nice to an idiot like this for so long, before her natural bitchiness surfaced.

The easiest thing was to keep Max talking about himself.

"So, tell me about your job?" Mel asked without thinking. A brief look of panic crossed Max's face, but he quickly righted himself.

"I work in computers."

"Do you? I got a computer myself last year. My friends finally managed to convince me to get one, and I have to admit the shopping on-line is so much fun," Mel quipped brightly.

Max visibly relaxed, and smiled back at Mel.

"I work for myself importing and exporting items through my own websites," Max announced to Mel grandly.

I bet you do, Mel thought.

".. and the best part is, that I never have to deal with anything other than the computer. It's all done remotely." Suddenly, it clicked as to how Max had accessed all of Mel's passwords, and the voice that she had thought she recognized.

Mel had never spoken to Max other that the occasional hello in the hall way, so she hadn't remembered his voice at the time of the 'Computer Technician' phony phone call.

"Are you Okay there Mel, you look a little peaky?"

Max interrupted her suddenly swirling thoughts. Mel looked up at Max, and then over his shoulder to see Nick making his way over to them.

"I'm fine," She had to force a smile back at Max.

Max looked taken back at the evil glint in her smile, when suddenly Nick appeared and pulled up a chair, sitting down at the small table.

"So I guess you're wondering why someone like Mel has bothered to notice someone like you," Nick said, by way of introduction.

Max looked from Nick to Mel, his eyes narrowed, giving him a beady eyed cabbage doll impression.

"Do you know this guy?"

Max looked at Mel questioningly.

"Yup," Mel offered nothing else, and sipped her drink quietly.

"Mel, what's this guy doing here?" Max asked Mel, with growing suspicion on his face.

"You stole money from my account and made it look like Mel had done it, dumb arse," Nick certainly got straight to the point.

"That wasn't very nice of you," Mel added. "Pretending to be a computer technician to gain my information, pretty low."

"Seriously? You fell for that?" Nick asked Mel in amazement.

"Are you on my side or not?" Mel glared at Nick, and he looked embarrassed for a brief moment.

"You need to turn yourself in and tell people what you did," Nick said back to Max.

Max glanced from one to the other to see if they were serious.

Then his piggy little face split into a wide grin.

"Turn myself in? To who?" Max laughed, then farted, and laughed harder. "The police have nothing and neither do you."

"Nope. So you need to give the police all the information to convict you. You need to let them prosecute you," Nick said firmly. "Otherwise, things are going to get nasty."

"Nasty huh? Anything you two have in mind for me, I'm sure the police can deal with. Because unlike you, I have a clue about how things work with the law. I've done nothing wrong, but if the two of you have any ideas of bugging me... well I won't hesitate to inform the police about how you are harassing me," Max smirked at them.

"How did the last trip to the doctors go?" Mel asked suddenly. "Did you get your lab tests back?"

Max froze in his seat for a moment.

"Now I know what you're up to, and you haven't got a chance against me. I won't be falling for any ex-lax brownies again." He glared at them.

Mel leaned forward in her seat.

"Good, because I haven't had a chance to extend my game in years."

This didn't have quite the intended outcome, because both men were now openly staring at her chest.

Stupid low cut shirt.

"Oh Ick. Grown up, you dicks."

Mel decided she'd had enough clever banter for one day, and she stood up and collected her purse.

"Don't go to the police, makes it more fun for me. But in future you should learn not to pick on the techno-logically challenged."

Mel walked out the cafe, leaving the two of them staring at her tight fitting jeans. Looking back to each other Max was the first to break the silence.

"She's hot when she's mad, but it looks like luscious there backed the wrong horse. Because you are going down." Max said.

Nick stood up. "Grow up, you dick. No wonder you can't get a girl."

Nick walked out of the cafe quickly, hoping to catch up with Mel, as she walked home.

A few minutes later Mel realized she was being followed by Nick.

"When you've finished admiring the view back there, you can speak to me," Mel said a few minutes later.

"Okay," Nick smiled, as he continued walking behind her for another minute, before trotting quickly to catch up.

They continued in silence back to Mel's place.

"So… we gave Max the option to turn himself in, and he didn't do it. Not a big surprise there, but what do you have planned now?" Mel asked, when they got back inside her apartment.

"His social life doesn't include much, but he does have a lot of time invested in on-line gaming which he is about to lose. Along with all of his virtual toys." Nick smiled lovingly at the laptop computer in front of him. "He also likes vintage comics and collectibles."

"Are you sure that will annoy him?" Mel had to ask. "Losing some imaginary stuff on the Internet?"

Nick gaped at her. "Imaginary stuff? He has spent over two thousand hours on just one game, and I'm going to delete all of them."

"Well yes, but it's just a game," Mel said, sceptically. "And what are virtual toys? That isn't some kind of sex thing is it? Because yuck and ick."

Nick looked at her with incredulity. "No, it is an on-line world, where you can buy houses, cars and clothes."

Mel looked at Nick for a long moment in puzzlement.

"But ... why bother? Why not just walk out the door, and get a real life?"

Mel finally asked in disbelief. "You know, I don't think that sort of thing will last anyway."

"Why not?" Nick asked.

He realized that Mel was one of those people who would never understand the gaming world.

Mel paused for a moment, then started looking for her pen and paper before answering. "It's a built in genetic blocker. You would never be able to produce offspring from it."

"You think everything is about sex don't you? Sometimes it's about low self-esteem too." Nick said, thinking of the type of person who invested a lot of time in those games, and wondering how many hours he had clocked himself. "Hmm… really," Mel thought about Max for a moment, tapping her pen on a pad of paper.

"Can you find his parents or family details for me?" She eventually asked.

"Yes... why?" Nick asked, curious at the abrupt change in conversation.

"Because I want to have a nice long talk with his mother, if she lives nearby," said Mel, thinking of an earlier plan of revenge.

"Why? Not that I'm not okay with that," Nick added quickly "But it seems kind of harsh to tell on him to his mother."

"Really?! You think *I'm* harsh? You stole my life savings on a whim, and you think a little embarrassment is too harsh?" Mel was stunned.

"What about when I had a week's worth of groceries in my cart, a queue behind me and no way to pay for it?"

"Well, it's just not something I would do," Nick replied, looking uncomfortable. This was obviously against some kind of guy code, Mel thought.

Too bad.

Mel wasn't a guy, and this was personal, damn it!

"Well, I should hope not." Mel said, with an evil smile spreading across her face. "Because I'm going to pretend to be his old girlfriend. The best part is, he will let me do it, because he won't want to admit what he did to his mother."

Mel had a rough idea of Max's reactions to the 'Tell Mummy Plan' thanks to her working on getting a degree in psychology when she was younger.

She had flunked out and gone into insurance, when she realized how boring it would be to listening to other people complain about their lives all day long.

Nick smiled broadly at Mel as he walked to the kitchen to make himself a coffee, seeing as he didn't get a chance for one at the cafe. He would never have thought of that approach.

"There's food in the fridge if you want it," Mel called out.

"Yes, but can I eat it without having any adverse effects?" Nick joked back.

Mel snickered.

"You're fine, I forgive you. I doubt I can get Max to eat anything else of mine now."

"Really, I'm forgiven? Since when?"

"Since I saw how much money Max took from you, and all the other people he ripped off. I can't believe the police are so crap at this type of theft. I would have done worse to Max, if I was in your shoes."

"You mean I haven't seen your A-Game yet?" Nick walked over to the couch and stood beside Mel, but a few inches too close for Mel's peace of mind.

"Nope I've been strictly law abiding and reasonable so far," Mel said backing away a little from him.

Mel was feeling way too comfortable with Nick and she wasn't sure that was a good thing just yet. They hadn't even kissed and yet she couldn't stop thinking about him.

"You know, the sexually aggressive scare tactics are running a little dull, Mel." Nick stepped closer again, backing her into the couch seat so that she sat down heavily. "I actually think you're afraid of intimacy."

Mel raised an eyebrow at him.

"Not sex," Nick clarified. "But allowing yourself to care and having someone to care for."

Mel suddenly felt like she was ten years old again, being lectured to, as he stood over her.

Standing up made the situation only slightly better, Mel had to stand right against Nick's chest and looked straight into his deep, laughing eyes.

"The day I'm afraid of a man like you," Mel said slowly and carefully. "Is the day you can put me to bed with a shovel."

Nick kept looking down at her for a moment, then his smile faded a little as he realized she was serious and he took half a step back.

"Fine then," Nick said softly, his eyes were still smiling. "You win."

Mel had to physically resist the urge to step forward into him.

It would be a bad idea to do this right now, Mel told herself. They had work to do and a man to emasculate.

Taking a jagged breath and stepping away, Mel did her best to ignore Nick's chuckle, and went to the bathroom for a powder break. Five minutes later, when she emerged, Nick was nowhere to be seen and Mel didn't know whether to be relieved or annoyed at herself.

Chapter 7

Di and Sal called in to Mel's apartment that night, and they all hung out on the couch in front of the TV for the first time in weeks. Watching the short clips of the party Mel had a few weeks before, they giggled at the table surfing and then began discussing the Nick and Max situation.

"So, any progress with Nick?" Di was straight to the point as usual. "Also, we were wondering what his last name was and where he worked?"

"We are working on dealing with Max, so no progress. And why do you want his details?" Mel knew her friends far too well to simply give out information

"Cause if he breaks your heart, we are going to rain unholy fire down on him," Sal said simply. Friends were the best sometimes.

Mel thought about it.

"I think Nick is safe as far as that goes. He's a bit of a geek himself and I'm pretty sure I have the upper hand most of the time."

"Really? This guy didn't seem to break a sweat when he ruined your life before, but now you're not worried?" Sal observed, critically.

"When do we get to meet him?" Di chipped in. "I want to know what he looks like."

"Maybe when this thing with Max is over, but not yet." Mel mulled the idea over. "I don't want to scare him off."

They ordered pizza as they talked into the night, and eventually decided that if Mel got serious about Nick, she would introduce him to them.

But if not, then he would be left alone.

It was close to midnight before Mel and Sal started to yawn and Di started to jingle the car keys.

"Try not to worry about him being in my house so

much, honey. He's probably just desperate for female company," Mel laughed as they got ready to leave.

"That's right," Sal snickered. "Doesn't he work in IT?"

"I'm still not giving you that info." Mel smiled, "G'night ladies."

Mel shut the door behind them with a sigh, and fell into her bed two minutes later with relief.

"Come on in, Nick. It's open," Mel called out the next day.

Mel felt tired and scratchy from a bad night's sleep, full of half-remembered and oh so hot, dreams.

She was feeling out of sorts and in no mood to play happy hostess to Nick, however cute he looked, it just made her feel worse.

Nick looked like he had also had a lousy night, as he sulked in the door and straight to the kitchen. Mel noticed he was looking distantly uncomfortable with his shirt slightly un-tucked, and his collar not quite straight.

"Someone has signed me up for a year's subscription to *Gay Guys Monthly*." Nick scowled at Mel.

She cracked up laughing, her mood lightening almost immediately.

"Really? It wasn't me, but I wouldn't put it past my mother."

"It arrived at my work, and the other guys in the department are looking at me strange." Nick snarled back.

"Well, you hurt her baby girl. Consider it payback for the public humiliation I had to go through, just to get my rent and power money from her."

He glared at her for a minute before looking away.

"Did you realize that this entire living room is screaming 'Old Spinster Lady' with three cats?" Nick said, changing tack as he looked around him. Lack of sleep and too many cold showers had obviously put him in the mood for an argument with Mel. "If you want to catch a man, you really need to redecorate."

"I knew I was missing something,"

Mel smirked and walked over to the counter, pulling out a pen and paper.

"Thanks for the tip."

A moment later a large note was stuck to the fridge
Buy a Cat.

"You don't want a man in your life do you?" Nick asked Mel, incredulous.

"What? You think this apartment look is an accident?"

Mel looked at him with a wicked smile on her lips.

"Well, I don't want a permanent man, but feel free to stay over tonight if you want. Most of the time, I want a man to leave in the morning, and it's generally less hassle if he decides to leave rather than me having to kick him out."

Nick looked at her in a kind of admiration, mingled with horror. "So what if he decided to get serious? Hypothetically speaking,"

"If I wanted to 'get serious' with a man, then I would redecorate, and change the theme. But I think you can guess how many times that has happened," Mel snickered.

Both their moods seemed to lighten, as they talked and laughed together for the rest of the day.

Mel had to remind herself that this was definitely not dating with Nick.

It was just planning a great revenge on Max, nothing else.

It was Saturday again, and Mel had finally made the decision to lay down the last of her efforts to Max, before she made the effort to come up with anything new. She took a taxi to Max's mother's house, arriving at a cute row of houses in a typical suburban neighborhood. She arranged to have the taxi pick her up in an hour.

"Hi Max, guess where I am, you obnoxious little turd," Mel said into her cell phone.

"Like I care," Max sounded like he was about to hang upon her.

"Outside your mother's house," Mel said quickly, not wanting to lose the call. "I thought I would give you a fair shot at explaining yourself to her, before I did."

"What?" Max spluttered down the line. "You are seriously nuts. She'll never believe you. And how did you find out where she lives?"

Mel could feel the warm fuzzy feelings in her stomach all over again.

"How are the on-line games, and virtual worlds going?" She asked smiling.

There was a brief pause.

"I'll be there in half an hour."

The line went dead.

Mel played on her phone while she waited for Max to arrive. Thirty minutes later, Max's new Mini coup pulled up beside Mel and he got out. Some takeaway food wrappers fell out the car and flew away as he shut the door tight against the rest of the rubbish and beeped the car locked.

His car looked new but it also looked as though it needed a really good clean.

Mel looked at Max with distaste, the cheese balls he had been eating had stained around his mouth and fingers. In his haste to get here he hadn't put a jacket on.

Mel sighed, and pushed away from the lamp post, undoing the zip of her jacket but not quite revealing a white 'baby on board' t-shirt underneath.

"Last chance Max. Go straight to the police station right now or reap the consequences."

""No one is going to believe you." Max drew himself up, so that he was nearly tall enough to look in Mel's eyes. "Least of all my own mother."

"Really?" Mel asked. "She knows what a little darling you are and how you never do anything wrong?"

"Seriously? You are going to tell on me to my mother?"
Max laughed, but a slight twitch was developing near one
of his eyes.

"Hell, no. That's a little too predictable." Mel walked up to
the door, and knocked loudly.

The door was opened quickly, to an older woman with
graying hair in tight curls, who had obviously been
watching from the window. Staring at Mel for a moment,
Max's mother quickly recovered, and shot them lightning
fast smile, so fleeting if Mel had blinked, she would have
missed it.

"Hello Maximus. I do wish you would have called first, I
hate the thought of new people coming over for the first
time, and the house not being tidy," Max's mother said,
stiffly.

Mel felt that was more a personality trait of hers than a
reaction to them.

"Oh no, the house is fine," Mel smiled, walking past her
and straight into the house.

Mel did her best to gush niceness and treated the older
woman to a warm bear hug, then walked into the lounge.

"I'm mean, it's we're family now anyway. Gosh, this
house is so nice, how much do you think it's worth?" She
looked about her.

The decor was baby pink and scarlet with plastic covers
on the furniture and fluorescent bright runners on every
small table. Mel was tempted to take notes in case the
pastels and quilts ever stopped turning men away.

"Mother, this is my neighbor, Mel," Max stated quickly.
"We really didn't mean to disturb you. We'll be going."

"It's fine, Maximus." The older woman looked from Max
to Mel with obvious delight. "Did you say you're part of
the family?"

"Yup, and I'm sooo glad he's letting me tell you. I wasn't
sure he would be able to wait."

Mel took off her jacket, and slung it over the plastic

covered couch. Maximus and his mother stared at her t-shirt for a long moment, before Max's eyes narrowed and he looked up to Mel's innocent wide-eyed expression. The shirt was blue, with baby booties and 'BABY ON BOARD' in bold lettering across it.

"She's not pregnant Mum, and we aren't together," Max said quickly composing himself, while his mother looked at Mel's shirt, transfixed by the words.

Mel's eyes filled with tears as she let her face show her devastation at Max's remarks.

"Max! I told you before. I don't know how many times I can say it before you believe me. I wasn't with anyone else, there was only ever you."

"Maximus!" The older lady seemed to regain her power of speech.

"I know Mum, but trust me, she's lying." Max stuttered in what he probably thought was a firm voice.

"First he says I'm not pregnant. Then he says it's not his. I just don't get how you can be so cruel to me, Max. I thought we had something special. I know I'm not perfect Max, but who is? I had thought we'd make a good match."

Mel looked at Max, then at his mother and sat down heavily on the couch with her head in her hands hiding her face as she smirked and waited for the blood to rush to her face and make it look all blotchy.

Mel could never cry on cue, but this usually made her look like she had been.

"I never thought you would throw me out, pregnant. I really thought we could be happy together," Mel sniveled into her knees.

"Max!" His mother said, pulling herself out of her stunned trance. "How could you do this to her! You know what a hard time we had when your father left! Now you would do this to someone else?"

"My name is Elsie, but you can call me Mother if you like darling." She leaned down, and gave Mel a reassuring hug.

Mel quickly hugged her back for a long moment, and poked her tongue out at Max over Elsie's shoulder.

"Now, don't you worry about a thing darling. You can live with me until Maximus comes to his senses and sees this for the blessing it is," Elsie said quickly.

"Oh thank you so much. But my apartment is right beside Max's, and I think it would be easier for us to work things out if I stayed closer for now. But thank you so much, you have no idea how good it is to have someone on my side for once."

Mel sniffed then smiled in relief at the sweet woman. "Well, if you're sure, but don't you forget you can come back anytime you want." Elsie glared at her son.

"Thanks so much," Mel sat up a little straighter in her seat. "I know this is a lot for you to get all at once, but I hope we can be friends as well as family. For now though, I think I should be going." Mel stood up and faced Max.

"If you want a paternity test when the baby's born, I will be happy to give you permission. But please, just give us a chance to be a family. So at least we can say we tried?" Max glared at Mel in silence as she quietly left the house, waving a shy goodbye to Elsie.

The yelling match between them started before Mel had walked out of the driveway.

Mel laughed all the way home.

Chapter 8

The next day Mel happened to be walking downstairs to work, when she saw Elsie trying to haul two large suitcases up the stairs.

"Hi. How are you Elsie?" Mel smiled delighted to see her. "Please let me take one of those."

"Oh. Thank you so much, Mel. They are easy to roll on with the little wheels, but pulling them upstairs is a bit harder than I thought it would be."

They chatted pleasantly, as they walked slowly up to Max's apartment.

When they reached the top Mel stepped back, and let Elsie knock.

The door swung open to a startled Max, who looked at the two women and his bloodshot eyes grew round with horror.

"Maximus, honey. I've decided to come and stay for a little while," Elsie informed Max, as she walked in. "So the three of us can have more time together."

Mel had to stop herself from laughing at the horrified expression on Max's face.

"I have to go to work now, but you have a great day Elsie and I'll see you later," Mel said good bye as Elsie smiled and shut the door.

Mel heard the two of them start arguing as she walked back downstairs to work.

Mel invited Nick over to review the fight, that night at her apartment after he had finished work.

Thanks to the cameras that Nick had installed, they could rewind and pause the action, to watch it when it suited them.

It was quickly becoming their new favorite reality TV show. Mel wondered if Nick would mind her showing her mother Regina, Sal and Di as well.

The girls still felt like Mel had let Nick off too lightly, and she was sure this footage would help put things in perspective for them.

"You can't just move in Mum! I'm not a kid anymore. This is my life! You can't be here."

"How on earth can you live like this? The mess, dirt and, oh my God, the smell!"

Max's mother obviously didn't come to visit very often.

Nick was waiting for Mel to finish making her drink, and had his eyes glued to the computer.

"I can't believe you could be so cruel," Nick said, looking up as she put her bag on the kitchen bench.

"It's just a variation on the original plan to get you back," Mel said to Nick's back.

"But you won't do that to me anymore, will you?" Nick asked, still looking at the screen, but his shoulders had gone stiff.

In the background, Mel could hear Elsie telling Max off for the state he kept his apartment in.

"Nope, your sweet nature and good looks persuaded me to take a different course of action."

Nick stood up and walked over to her, and Max was forgotten about for the moment.

"Is this sexual aggression thing another defense mechanism of yours?" Nick asked trying to call Mel's bluff.

Mel looked up at Nick and swallowed, but she really didn't have an answer that she could articulate.

"You need to get that debt collector over here now, before he can kick Elsie out," said Mel after a brief moment. "Or before she starts to pay the bills."

"OK." Nick backed off and walked over to his cell phone and sent a quick text off then he looked at Mel again. Mel said nothing to him and blushed as the silence expanded, busying herself at making coffee.

"Also, why do all the quilts and things have price tags on them?" Nick asked.

That was one question that Mel could answer with a smile.

"Because if I must throw all those stupid work parties and deal with colleagues who pretend like they are my best friends, just to keep my stupid job in this stupid economy, then I can at least be compensated."

A few minutes later, the tension in the room had thankfully dropped as they sat on the couch together and watched Max explain the debt collector at his door, to his mother.

The next day they had agreed to meet up and watch the feed from Max's apartment for a few hours. Mel made popcorn, and Nick brought expensive coffee from the cafe.

After opening the door to Nick, Mel quickly hurried him to sit down.

"They just started up again, watch... it's hilarious."

"Ahhhaaa... will you look at this? There is pee pee all around the toilet!"

"Relax it was just an accident. Some friends pranked me, by putting cling film over the toilet."

"Well you couldn't always aim when you left home, and even if it was a prank why on earth haven't you cleaned it up yet?"

He glared at his Mother for a moment.

"I've been busy working I was going to get around to it soon."

"Sure, just like the trash and the vacuuming," Elsie gave back, glare for glare.

Mel and Nick cracked up laughing at the screen.

"Can you believe these two?" Nick asked gasping for air.

"What is this in the toilet Mum?" Max yelled a few minutes later. "I do not have bad aim. I told you it was a prank."

Mel looked at Nick with a raised eyebrow. He shrugged and grinned at Mel, then he looked back at the screen.

"You think I want to take that risk? It's bad enough that I have to leave the toilet seat up for you. I'm not sitting in that!"

"I can't have a wine bottle cork in my toilet, Mum! What if I have friends over?"

"Then you can explain to them how to play 'Battle Piss,' and that the cork in the toilet with the ship drawn on it, needs to be sunk. Besides, when was the last time you had a friend over?"

Max took a deep breath, his face going an unhealthy red shade.

"I can't live like this, Mother. You have to go back to your own place."

Elsie looked back at Max for a moment, her face blank as she considered her options.

Then her face slowly crumbled and tears began to trickle down her cheeks.

"I want to be a part of your life honey, and your baby's life. You can't tell me to leave." She said as she began to cry in earnest.

"Okay, you can stay for a while, please stop crying. But

you have to remember that I'm a grown man now. And there is no baby."
"I will give you more space, darling I promise."

"Aw, they're hugging, how cute" Mel smiled viciously.
"It won't last." Nick frowned.
"I know, but I'm enjoying the build-up."

"Mum, what happened to my comic collection?" Max asked, a few minutes later in a strangled voice.
"What?"
"My comic's, Mum. They were stacked up in the lounge in boxes."
"Oh, those boxes filled with old paper got thrown in the trash this morning with everything else, of course. Why you insist on keeping piles of old papers is beyond me."
Max stood up abruptly.
"Those were vintage comics in mint condition! Mum do you know what you've done?"
"I threw away a load of trash, is what I did."
"I can't believe this!" Max gasped for air. "HOW COULD YOU THROW AWAY $10,000.00 WORTH OF COMICS?"
"It was just old comic papers Maximus. Don't be so silly. Dinner is nearly ready, and I bet you haven't had a decent cooked meal in a while."
Max paused in his rant, food swiftly overtaking money in his priorities.
"What did you make?" he asked, apprehension filling his stomach.
"Vegetable gumbo. I saw the rubbish in the fridge and the pantry, and after I donated all the junk food to the local shelter, I went shopping. If you're going to be a father in a few months, you need to be able to run around, not waddle. It's a good thing I'm here to look after you."

"I hate vegetables! You know that!" Max saw the future staring at him. It was full of cleaning, healthy eating and early bedtimes. It looked like Hell. "And I am not going to be a father!"

"Vegetables are good for you, so you will eat them."

Mel and Nick collapsed into each other's arms roaring with laugher.

The next morning, Mel saw on the laptop that Max was heading down stairs with a mountain of laundry and decided to join him. Quickly gathering a few things, she threw them into the washing basket, and followed him down to the basement.

"How did you get her to do this?" Max yelled at Mel as soon as she walked in the laundry door.

"It really didn't take that much of a push; she wasn't liking the idea of her grandchild growing up so far away from her anyhow," Mel smiled back. Truthfully, she had been as surprised as he was that Elise had decided to move in. But it didn't hurt to take credit for it, and Mel was really enjoying Max's misery.

"She lives half an hour away and *you're not pregnant*!" Max yelled.

"Well, Elsie is here now, so get used to it," Mel stated.

"You know how to make this all stop."

"Confess to the police? No, way bitch," Max snarled. "You are going to pay for this."

His chubby face distorted in fury.

"Anything you do to me, I'll tell Elsie," Mel shot back.

"I haven't had a girlfriend in over five years, and even then it was just an Internet fling," Max hissed back.

Having had the full force of Max's gingivitis unleashed on her, Mel believed him completely.

"She doesn't believe you're pregnant with her grandchild."

"Really? Because she's been so kind to me."

Mel kept up the smile, a malicious glint came into her eyes. "Did you know she brought her knitting with her?"

"So?"

"Your mother is making bootees for the baby, so she must be keen on the idea." Mel smirked. "Face it Max, what other chance for grandkids has she got? She doesn't care if it's your baby or not, so long as she gets a grandchild."

He spluttered for a moment.

"How long do you think you can keep this up for?" Max asked. "She will realize you're lying when there's no baby bump."

"Then I will take a few days off work and have a miscarriage, and when you are being so callous about everything I'm going through, I'm going to recommend group counseling for the three of us," Mel said as straight faced as she could. Then she decided to go for the kill.

"So far, you have no games to play, no money to spend and no social life. If I can't make every second of your day a living hell, I'll make your mother do it for me. Turn yourself in and confess, chances are you only get a few months in jail and I'll be off your case, and your mother will have moved out. If you don't, I'm going to go to the next level, and start you downloading kiddy porn from the websites the police watch. You know what happens to pedophiles in prison? Confess to the robbery at the accountants, and using my Wi-Fi. Or things are going to get so much worse for you."

"You can't do that." Max sneered.

"Do you really want to take that chance?" Mel whipped back at him. She stared at him for a long moment, and his face slowly turned white before he stomped off, back up to his apartment.

Mel hummed a song to herself as she sorted her washing, after a few minutes she realized she was humming the tune, 'One way, or another, I'm going get you."

Chapter 9

Police Station Interview Room No 6 at 2pm the next day.

"I'm here to make a confession." Max looked at the officer, waiting patiently to be arrested.

They were seated in a small beige colored room at the police station, with one desk, two chairs and a small camera high up in the ceiling.

"And what are they?"

Officer Cane was bored, he had better things to be doing with his time than sitting listening to some short ugly crackpot confess to some fictional crimes. "Did you shoot JFK? Escape from Al Qaeda, or rob a bank?"

"No, dumb ass, I've committed cyber-crimes. Most of them you don't have laws against, but these ones you do."

Max took a sip of water then he laid out some papers on the table.

"Firstly, I set up an Internet website that you could buy fictional items from. Some people actually thought that it was real, can you believe it? Talk about dumb. I collected their money into an offshore account in the Philippines. When that started to dry up from all the bad reviews. I decided to look at other ways to make money, but I couldn't have the police after me. So I got some random people's information by pretending to be a computer technician, so I could ping their computers and hide my real location."

He paused for another sip of water.

"Then I broke into a local accountant's office on a Friday night. Pulled a long weekend of hard work to get everyone's credit cards maxed out by buying things on my websites, before the accountant realized that they had been broken into. I then had the money offshore to access any time I wanted. And no way for anyone to track me."

Max stopped for a moment.

Looking directly at the camera in the corner.

"You do know that the amount of effort you put into this, you could have made a legitimate business," Officer Cane said dryly, paying close attention now to Max and glancing at the files Max had put on the desk.

"Probably, but where's the fun it that?"

Max paused to look around the room again. Prison had to be better than living with his mother and that nut bar woman next door. He knew she had slipped another laxative into his food again, when she came to visit his mother the other day. God only knew what else she and her boy-friend had planned.

"So, if this plan was so great, what the hell are you doing here confessing to everything?" Officer Cane asked, looking through the files now with much more interest.

"Well, I didn't know that one of the guys from the accountants was a techno too, and he was pretty pissy that his credit cards had been maxed out. At first, he thought it was my neighbor, because I was using her Wi-Fi. But after a while, they both realized what I was up to and then…"

He looked up at the camera in the top corner of the room again.

"Are you okay?" Officer Cane asked, wondering why Max was watching the camera's so nervously.

"Yup, just making sure you're getting all this." Max tore his gaze back to the policeman.

"The neighbors then decided to make life a bit uncomfortable for me until I confessed everything, so here I am. I'm confessing to everything I did," Max finished.

"How did they do that?"

"Do what?" Max played for time for a moment.

"How did they make you confess?"

"Um, well… they made me aware of the people who have suffered so much, and I felt it was my duty to turn myself in."

Max closed his mouth with finality. Officer Cane had the distant feeling that he weren't going to get much more out of him.

"Can I stay here the night?" Max asked, thinking of the vegetable fritters his mother had been making for dinner. He hated the taste and they always gave him the runs

"Definitely."

Max sighed in relief.

Back at Mel's apartment, Mel and Nick high fived each other, grinning from ear to ear.

Nick had hooked up the computer to the TV so they could watch it on a bigger screen.

Watching the police video feed live was almost as good as being there in person, but in person they wouldn't have been able to eat popcorn and drinking lemonade while Max confessed, or be snuggled up close on the cozy couch together.

"I still can't believe we got him to do it," Mel said beaming. Success is always the best revenge, she thought to herself. Although she was mildly curious as to how Nick had gotten the police video and audio feed.

"Well, we seem to make a pretty good team," Nick smiled at her. "You asked me once how I knew all the computer stuff that I do?"

"Yes, and you didn't answer me, so I dropped it. You don't have to tell me." Mel was dying to know though.

"I worked for the New Zealand Ministry of Defense, in the IT department." Nick explained smiling.

An urge to wrap herself around him and pull him to the floor become irresistible. Mel looked up into his darkening blue eyes, as Nick stared back down. She knew that she could do a lot worse than letting a slightly geeky, sweet guy like him stay the night. Leaning back into his shoulder, she tilting her head back, loving the look in his darkening eyes.

The music of Barry White's "let's get it on,' floated around them.

They leaned in for a kiss…

Connect with Lynda Ruth Price at ...

Twitter https://twitter.com/LyndaRuthPrice

Facebook Lynda Ruth Price: Author

Other books by Lynda Ruth Price

The Classy Crimes Series #1

Mel's Revenge

You know all those annoying calls from people wanting to help 'fix' your computer?
And you know they are scams right?
Well, Mel didn't know, and now she's had her bank account emptied, her phone frozen and there is no help in sight.
But it's when she finds the source of her misery that the fun really begins.

The Classy Crimes Series #2
Cougar Files

Regina has everything. A multi-million dollar business to run. A new building to create. A cute new boyfriend to date, and now she even has her very own sinister stalker to run from. Will she find a white knight to rescue her, or will she pull on her big girl pants and do it herself?

The Classy Crimes Series #3
Wild Men
Bob wants out of the gang
Trouble is, this is HIS gang.
Will Bob get free and find the only woman he ever loved? How can he get out of the gang without pissing off everyone in it? Will he get to keep the money he has stashed away over the years without the gang the police or

the Tax department getting hold of it? or will he be just another broken down old biker left on the side of the road? Going straight has never been this hard.

The Classy Crimes Series #4
Disturbing Tales of Suburbia

This is a group of five short story's exploring a simple question.
What would you do if you could get away with it?
Killers lurk in every corner of the world. Everyone is capable of it. Sometimes it just depends on the circumstances. What kind of person are you, how far do you need to be pushed in order to retaliate?
Do not try this at home, but if you do – don't get caught.